THE THERAPIST #2

SHAMELESS

BESTSELLING AUTHOR

W.S. GREER

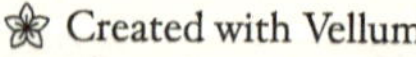 Created with Vellum

CRASH

essa ~

Have you ever felt like you were walking down a dark road? A road that doesn't feel like home. A road that is terrifying, and at the end of which you know there is nothing but impending doom. Have you ever felt like you were walking toward your end with every step you take? Well, that's how I've felt for far too long now, and today is the day the doom swallows me.

The office is beautifully decorated: hardwood floors, walnut wood furniture that meshes perfectly with the black and brown couch I find myself sitting on, and elegant art on the walls that isn't too distracting, but beautiful nonetheless. It's a comforting setting, which I especially appreciate at this moment, because I need all the comfort I can get.

Across from me is a man I never thought I would have to sit in front of, but after struggling to solve the puzzle on our own the past six months, we're here. His name is Dr. Malcolm Colson, and he's a relationship therapist. We've been seeing him for four weeks now, and although Dr. Colson is brilliant, I don't think we're making much progress. We're moving, but it doesn't feel like it's in the right direction. That's not Dr. Colson's fault, though, it's ours.

Sitting on the couch next to me is my boyfriend of the last two years, Brandon Stills. Brandon is a gorgeous man. He's just under six-feet tall, with short, perfectly manicured hair and a beard that's neatly trimmed. His hair is dark brown while his eyes are light brown, and he holds the confidence of a man two feet taller than he is. Brandon is in decent shape, as he hits the gym regularly, and he attracts plenty of attention from women, even when he's standing next to me. I always felt lucky to have him. Until I didn't.

Dr. Colson is a beautiful man in his own right. He's probably six-feet tall himself, but he's got a bit more to his frame than Brandon. Dr. Colson's shoulders are broader, and his chest grabs my attention through the fabric of his button-up shirt. He's probably two-hundred pounds to Brandon's one-seventy, and his skin has that luscious golden brown you get when you have interracial parents. His green eyes are impossible to ignore, and the confidence he emits is like a fog that engulfs you when you get too close to him. It's something I wish I could breathe in and use for myself, but since I can't, I've found myself leaning on Dr. Colson for support when we come here. He's been the best therapist I could ask for, and his skill is being put to the test.

I'm in the presence of two beautiful men, but I've never felt more uneasy and self-conscious. The air doesn't feel like it should. It's thicker, like the weight of the tension in the room is mixing with the oxygen and making it harder to breathe in. The comfortable couch doesn't feel as cozy as it did four weeks ago, and I feel as though I've run out of positive words to add to the conversation. I'm tired of it. I'm tired of him. I'm just so very tired of it all.

"You see, this is what I'm talking about," Brandon says. His words pull me out of my daze and roughly drag me back into the conversation I no longer want any part of. "See? She just goes to some happy place inside her head, and it's like I'm talking to myself. She doesn't want to listen to me. Jesus."

I look up and see Dr. Colson staring at me, his green eyes captivating me. He doesn't look angry, but then again he never does. He looks like he's trying to read me. It's like I'm an open book, but I'm written in a language he hasn't learned yet, so he's thumbing through the pages looking for words he recognizes so he can piece them together to make a complete sentence.

I've been fascinated by Dr. Colson's ability to pay close attention to us. He listens better than any man I've ever met, and he uses the information to give us sound advice that I believe could work if we were two people who were still invested in working it out, which I'm not sure we are anymore. Dr. Colson has earned my trust and respect. I only wish Brandon would shut the fuck up so Dr. Colson could earn his.

"Okay, you're frustrated, Brandon," Dr. Colson says, his voice low and commanding. "And I like that you're communicating today, instead of holding it all in. However, your communication can't be powered by assumptions. I don't think Tessa doesn't want to listen to you. I think what's more likely is that your main concern is talking and getting your point across, rather than reading your girlfriend's body language and nonverbal clues. From what I'm seeing—and please correct me if I'm wrong, Tessa—Tessa is shutting down. She looks drained. Brandon, have you asked Tessa how she feels about all of this?"

I don't look over at him, but I hear Brandon let out an exasperated breath before speaking.

"I don't have to ask her anything," Brandon says. "I can tell from the look on her face that she's somewhere else in her head, and that's fine with me, because I can go some-where else in mine."

Now it's my turn to sigh. When I do, both men in the room turn their eyes to me. I've been quiet throughout the entire session today, choosing instead to let Brandon get out whatever bullshit he wants to say. Maybe I'd feel compelled to speak up if I felt like Dr. Colson believed a single word slithering out of Brandon's mouth, but I can tell he doesn't. He looks disinterested, which is the mirror reflection of how I feel.

However, everybody has a tipping point. Usually, when Brandon starts off on one of his long venting sessions, I just let him vent. My mother taught me not to say anything when I don't have anything positive to add to the conversation, but that is getting to be too much of a task, because not only am I tired, I'm fed up.

"Tessa, is there something you'd like to add?" Dr. Colson asks. Those green eyes of his glare at me, telling me that the therapist has given me an in, and that I should take advantage of the opportunity.

I turn to Brandon and shake my head. "That was a joke, right?"

Brandon frowns. "What?"

"What you just said about going somewhere else in your head," I continue. "Brandon, you don't need to go somewhere else in your head, because you literally leave all the time. You're always out doing something else. That's what brought us here in the first place. You don't touch me anymore, and that's because you're always gone."

"You're mad that I don't touch you?" Brandon tries to strike back. "That's so dumb, Tessa. How do you expect me to touch you when I'm out trying to make something of myself? I'm out there trying to make it big, while you're content being a veterinary assistant, working at your father's clinic. You might be okay with a normal, boring life, but I'm not. I'm out there trying to become somebody in this world.

"And if we're being honest, when we do get to spend time together, you don't even seem happy to be with me. Maybe I'm physically distant, but you're mentally distant. It's like you're constantly thinking about whether or not you even want to be with me anymore. You're never satisfied. Like, when we have sex, you look dispassionate and detached. When I ask you what you want me to do, you tell me you don't know, but you act mad that I don't know either. What am I supposed to do with that? How am I supposed to satisfy you when you don't even know what you want?"

I steal a glance at Dr. Colson, who's writing furiously on his yellow legal pad, and I'm dying to know what he thinks about all of this. When he's done writing, though, he doesn't speak. Dr. Colson is all about open communication. He's been harping on it from the moment we walked into his office, so when Brandon and I get into verbal spats, Dr. Colson seals his lips and picks up his pen, but he rarely interjects. He lets us work it out, unless he sees that we can't work it out on our own.

"Don't get mad at me for being driven, Tessa," Brandon continues, annoyance walking hand in hand with his every word. "I don't have a family-owned business to attach myself to. My father doesn't have a clinic for me to work at. I have to make it on my own. Nobody handed my skills to me. I became a music producer on my own."

"Oh, God. Here we go again," I spit out with a huff.

"Oh, fuck you," Brandon snaps. "Yes, I'm proud of the fact that I'm a music producer, and I'm proud of the fact that a band I produce and manage has booked a gig in D.C. this weekend. You can act like it's no big deal all you want, but this band is about to go sing songs that I produced the music to, playing a gig that I booked for them. That's a big deal to me, and it should be to you, too. You're just jealous that I'm about to become rich and famous, and you're going to be stuck working at Milton Animal Clinic under the shadow of your parents your entire fucking life, because I swear I'll leave you behind if you don't shape up. That's right. If you don't figure yourself out really quickly, you're going to lose out on me."

"God, you're a fucking asshole," I blurt, as I snap my head toward Brandon. "Nobody gives a fuck about that band. American Armpits is the dumbest band name I've ever heard, and they'll never amount to anything more than they are now. Attach yourself to those losers at your own peril, Brandon."

"Goddamn it, when did you become such a bitch?" Brandon barks.

"All right, all right, I think we need to reel it in," Dr. Colson speaks up with his hand in the air like a boxing referee. "You guys know I'm all about communication, and I can appreciate both of you opening up, but we need to try to keep it civil. We have to express our emotions without reverting to name-calling or putting words into each other's mouths. It's okay to be emotional, but you have to keep it from becoming hostile. If you two can't do that, then this road we're traveling on will become much more difficult to navigate. When you can't express yourselves without resorting to insults, and intentionally trying to bring each other down and hurt each other's feelings, that's a sign of a much deeper issue. When all you have left for each other is contempt and outrage, you have to ask yourselves an essential question. Do you even like each other anymore?"

In the time that Dr. Colson was letting us argue while he jotted notes, he came up with his best and toughest question yet, and I don't know the answer. I don't know if it's that I don't like Brandon anymore, or if it's that I don't know *myself* well enough to like who *I* am.

CHAPTER TWO

~ Tessa ~

The sound in the room is vacuumed out, and the cold silence left behind is blaring. The three of us sit awkwardly now. Dr. Colson's eyes move back and forth between Brandon and me, never settling on either of us. No one speaks. Within the stillness is the answer, hanging there like a vine, dangling back and forth between all of us.

Brandon and I don't look at each other. The anger has risen too high now, and neither of us can see over it. It's blocking our view of the things we hold dear about each other, and I don't know if there's any more progress to be made today, but Dr. Colson isn't one to give up. He takes pride in his ability to bring people together, and give couples a fighting chance. I can tell he takes this as a challenge, and he's determined to win. I'm just not sure if there is any victory to be had in this game Brandon and I are playing.

Dr. Colson lets out an exhausted sigh, before tossing his notepad onto the wooden desk between us.

"Okay," he begins, his voice coming out as calmly as possible. "We have to remember why we're here. You're not the first couple who has come in here and had arguments. That's what therapy is for. You're supposed to resolve issues that you're emotionally attached to. It's stressful and difficult, but we get through it together."

Brandon keeps his eyes trained on the hardwood floor, but I maintain eye contact with Dr. Colson as he goes on.

"No matter what, speaking up is always the best idea," Dr. Colson lectures. "We have to use our words, but we also have to remember not to be disrespectful, because no one wants to engage in a conversation where they feel disrespected. I can see that today is an emotional day for both of you, but nonetheless, I'm proud of you. This is our fourth session together, and it's the first time both of you have communicated openly. We've had days where only Tessa was able to open up, and days where only Brandon spoke, but you both communicated today, and that's great. Even if it got a little testy, it's always good when both parties can communicate.

"Now, I know I've floated a question that's difficult to answer, but I think it's important that we end today's session as best we can. Sometimes, the best way might not be the easiest way. It might not be the way that makes you happiest right now either. The answer to the question, though, is a crucial step in how the three of us will proceed.

"Sometimes, when we love each other, we forget to *like* each other. We forget to enjoy each other's company, and we forget what brought us together in the first place. There can be love deep inside, but if we don't like each other, it's really hard to continue. So, I think both of you need to think deeply on this question and see what answer comes up. If you can't answer right here and now, that's fine, but let's give it a try. Tessa, do you still *like* Brandon?"

My heart feels like it just got into a car wreck and went flying out the window, leaving me stunned inside the damaged vehicle, staring blankly at the destruction around me. I don't know how to answer because I feel like I can't even think right now.

How did it all come to this? Brandon and I were good two years ago. When we first met, we laughed all the time and wanted to spend every minute together. We had sex a lot, like most new couples do, and the sight of him walking into the room put a smile on my face.

I remember the good times like they were yesterday, and I don't even know when all of that stopped. I don't know when his pursuit of a music career became this overbearing thing that ran roughshod over our relationship. I don't know when his ego got so big and his perception of me became so ugly. I don't know when we started to resent each other. I don't know when I started questioning whether or not Brandon was even my type. I have no idea when all of this began, but I feel like it's so far gone now, there's no turning back. No matter how much therapy we go through, we won't be able to spark the flame again.

Before I know what hit me, there are tears gliding down my face. I hate crying, but I do it so often these days, it's the only thing in my life that feels familiar. The stream of tears doesn't stop, and Brandon exhales next to me, frustrated at the sight of his girlfriend weeping once again.

"Tessa," Dr. Colson says to me. "Tears are always telling. They have a meaning behind them, so if you can, I'd like you to try to speak to that. What are you feeling right now?"

"I don't fucking know," I snip, not at Dr. Colson, and not even at Brandon. Maybe I'm snipping at myself for being so unaware. I take a deep breath and try to gather my thoughts so I can speak coherently. "I'm just very confused. My whole life, I've gone along with things that I wasn't sure about. I always had people pushing me, telling me what to do, and it's gone on for so long that I don't know what *I* like. I just feel confused all the time."

"Oh, and that's *my* fault?" Brandon explodes with raised arms.

"I didn't say it was your fault," I fire back. "But you're here and it affects you, too. It has affected you. Maybe that's why you allowed yourself to become so distant from me. Maybe you could sense that I'm unsure about us... that I'm unsure about what I want."

"Wow. Well, there it is," Brandon barks, still in his feelings. "You just said it, didn't you, Tessa? You're unsure about us. You've *been* unsure about us. That's it right there. Is that why you didn't answer when he asked if you still like me?"

"You didn't answer either, Brandon!" I bellow, as the tears pouring from my eyes multiply.

"Oh geez. Fine, I don't fucking know if I like you or not, Tessa. I don't know. There, does that make you happy? All I know is that I'm on the verge of greatness, and I don't want to feel like I'm being dragged down by some neurotic, confused, unpleasable woman who's going through some sort of crisis. We used to be good together, but now I think I've changed. You've changed, too, and I just don't know anymore. I don't know if I like you or not. I love who you used to be when we first started going out. At least you were fun back then."

Dr. Colson lets out another sigh, and I know he's frustrated with how ugly this session has become. We're not supposed to insult each other, but it seems that's all Brandon can do right now.

"Do you still love me?" I ask with a trembling voice.

Brandon looks at me with a deep furrow in his brow. "You're doing that on purpose," he says.

"Doing what?"

"Trying to make me look bad," he answers. "You're sitting

over here talking about how you're not sure about this and that, but you ask me if I still love you as if I'm not allowed to be confused, too. If I say I don't love you, I look like an asshole. I'm the asshole in the room if I say no."

"This isn't about looking good or bad, Brandon," I try to explain the best I can with tears and emotion overtaking my face and voice. "I just want the answers we both need."

"Bullshit, you're trying to embarrass me, Tessa. I won't have it. Honestly, I'm sick of this bullshit. I think that's enough *therapy* for one day. I'm done. Fuck this."

"Brandon, please don't leave," Dr. Colson pleads, but Brandon is already up and walking toward the door. "This isn't healthy, Brandon. You can't make progress if you give up."

"Fuck your progress," Brandon says behind a scoff, and he doesn't slow down a single step as he walks out of the door.

Dr. Colson and I sit there for a moment, neither of us saying a word. This hasn't been easy for any of us, but today is the first time it feels like we're putting a Band-Aid over a gunshot wound. I've been with Brandon for two years, and the idea that we might not make it sends shockwaves rippling through me, and I'm shaken into heavy sobs. Dr. Colson pushes a box of tissues over to my side of the table, and I take one, bringing it to my face only to cry into it.

"It's unfortunate that he left," Dr. Colson says. I can hear both the sympathy and annoyance in his voice.

"I'm sorry," I blurt through ragged breathing, as I stand up to follow Brandon out. We drove here together, so I have to go, but my embarrassment is also ushering me out of the room. "I don't know when he became so angry. I'm just really sorry, Dr. Colson, on behalf of both of us."

Dr. Colson stands up and walks over to me. He lowers his head so we're face to face and making direct eye contact.

"You should never have to apologize on behalf of someone

else," he says. "Brandon is the one who should apologize for his behavior, not you. You can't control what he does or how he acts. You've been a great patient, Tessa. You're strong, and you care. You're just struggling through something a lot of people have difficulty with, and that's knowing and accepting who you are, without considering outside opinions. That can be very hard to do when you feel the weight of people's judgement putting pressure on you. But, no matter what happens next for you two, I'm here to talk if you need me. All you have to do is call. I hope to see you back here next week."

I don't know how to respond. The tears are too thick and my emotions are running too wild. As Dr. Colson escorts me to the door to his office, I simply nod at him, and step over the threshold into a world of uncertainty.

CHAPTER THREE

~ Tessa ~

The ride home was quiet—just the sound of the engine and breathing. We didn't even look at each other, and once we made it back to my place, Brandon only stopped in the driveway long enough for me to climb out, then he drove away without as much as a peek in my direction. We don't live together, so he decided to go back to his place, which was probably for the best. Over the next two days, not a single text was sent to my phone from him, nor did he receive one from me.

In our two days apart, I took time off from work and sat in my apartment alone. It was all I wanted to do, and the words of Dr. Colson kept playing in my head like a sad song on repeat. *You're struggling with knowing and accepting who you are without considering outside opinions.* He's never been more right, but in my time alone, the only thing I could focus on was my own confusion.

I still don't know how we got here, or where I'm supposed to go next. Nothing has changed for me since we left Dr. Colson's office, so when Brandon called and asked if he could come over, I didn't do anything different from what I'd normally do. I told him he could come.

When I open the door, Brandon stands there in a white T-shirt and blue jeans. He's comfortable, but he doesn't look happy to see me. He looks miserable, actually. Has he been stressing about how we got to this point the same way I have? I smile when I see him, but he doesn't return the gesture.

"Hi," he says with a blank face.

"Hey. How have you been?" I ask.

"Can I come in? I feel like we should talk," he replies, which is out of the norm. Usually, Brandon doesn't ask to come inside, he just does. He's stayed over for a whole week without leaving before. He's usually over so often, I feel like my apartment is *our* apartment. The change lets me know our discussion will be a serious one that involves just as much change as Brandon asking to come in.

I open the door and let Brandon glide past me. I can't remember the last time I opened this door and we didn't greet each other with a kiss and a hug, but the changes keep coming as I follow him into my living room, where he sits on the loveseat across from my couch. I take a seat and grab a pillow for me to hold in anticipation of where this conversation will go.

"Listen," Brandon begins. "I don't want this to take a long time. I don't want to drag it out, because I think we've done enough talking in that therapist's office. We've done enough arguing and finger-pointing, and quite honestly, Tessa, I'm over it. Aren't you?"

In the back of my mind, I feel a tinge of relief. Maybe this conversation won't be as bad as I expected. Is he here to tell me he just wants to go back to how we used to be? Would I be happy about that? Is that what I want, or am I ready to conform to whatever he wants, and what everybody around me expects?

"Yes, I am," I reply. "I'm tired of all the arguing and blaming each other. I *know* my mother is tired of me crying to her. She's told me as much. It's all been very exhausting."

"Yeah, it has. That's a great word for it. Exhausting." Brandon sighs and lowers his eyes to the floor, and the relief I felt vanishes, replaced by a heavy feeling in my gut. "Yes. I'm exhausted, Tessa. In fact, I'm completely drained. I've reached the end of my rope, and it's your fault. You've been like a concrete block attached to my ankles while I try to swim to happiness and success. You're pulling me down with all your insecurities and self-doubt, and I don't want to be anchored to you any longer. I can't sit back and allow myself to drown because of you, Tessa."

My heart plunges. My breathing stops. My head spins, and my mouth pinches shut. This is it. He's about to deliver the final blow—the ultimate change.

"American Armpits just booked another show," Brandon presses forward, his eyes finally rising to meet mine. His eyes are filled with confidence, mine with tears that haven't had the decency to fall, blurring my vision instead. "This show is in New York, and it's all because of the song I produced for them. It's going to be the first song on the demo they're about to record. Plus, they want me to produce another track on the demo. It's all about to happen for them, and they want me to be their full-time manager and producer. It's all happening with this group. The more exposure they get with the songs I'm working on, the more in demand I'll be. I'm going to make it, and I don't have time to slow down and wait for you."

"Wow," I whisper, finally finding my voice. "So, you're dumping me." It's a statement, not a question, but Brandon answers anyway.

"Yes, I am," he says with a head nod. "I think it's for the best, Tessa. You're in a weird spot internally right now, and the last thing I need is to have to deal with your resentment as I make my dreams come true, and you struggle to please your mother. So, I think we should go our separate ways."

I feel torn inside. I'm being dumped by the guy I've been dating for two years, and not just that, I'm being insulted as well. I'm shocked that Brandon's trash ass friends are actually booking shows here on the east coast. I'm in disbelief that the song Brandon played for me by American fucking Armpits is actually gaining traction. That song sucked! The band sucks! I feel like this is supposed to be a nightmare, but it's more like a scary movie parody where I want to laugh when I'm supposed to be screaming. However, even with all of that coursing through my veins, I can't stop myself from crying.

The tears in my eyes finally start to fall, and Brandon lets out his signature sigh—the one he goes to when he feels uncomfortable in the presence of a woman's emotions. I stare at him, unsure of what to say, and he stares back. I can't find any words, so I just look at him and watch as Brandon's face shifts into something more angry.

"You don't have anything to say?" he asks, and I know if I try to talk, I'll just cry more. So, I give him nothing more than a shrug. "Wow. After two years, you've got nothing to say. I see how it is. Well, that tells me all I need to know, Tessa. Seriously, you've got nothing?"

I wrack my brain searching for the right thing to say. I know my mother would want me to plead with him, and my friends would expect me to. But how do I feel? What do I want? I'm not sure I've ever asked myself that question. The words I choose to settle on are the ones I want to say most. *My* words.

"I'm not going to fight to hang on to someone who doesn't want me, Brandon," I tell him, just as I reach up and wipe my tears away. "I'm tired of feeling confused about what

I want, and I think it's time I embrace my own desires for a change. And the truth of the matter is, I think I have an answer to Dr. Colson's question. It's *no*. I don't like you anymore. I feel like I've been wearing a mask my entire life, only showing the world what I think it wants to see. I'm so tired of wearing that mask. So tired of trying to find the right thing to say. I'm done with it, so it's fine. Do what you want. Good luck with your band."

Brandon stares at me like I'm a stranger. He blinks five or six times before bringing himself to his feet and hovering above me while I look up at him. I don't even want to escort him to the door, so I'm not going to.

"Fine," he says with a careless shrug. "Yeah, good luck to you too, Tessa, with... whatever the hell you're going to do. Good luck finding a guy with more promise than me. I'll be on the road with my band, the same band you said was trash, and you'll be here, struggling with the trash barrel of men from Dover while you let your mother fail at playing match-maker for the rest of your life."

"Eat shit, Brandon," I snip.

"Whatever. Goodbye, Tessa."

Brandon turns on his heel and walks out the door, and I don't do anything to stop him, because for the first time in my life, I made a decision for myself. I did what I wanted. I hope it's a trend I can continue. However, when this gets back to my mother, the thing I'll want to do next is hide under a rock. For now, I think I'll just enjoy crying my final tears for my dead relationship, and think about how to be stronger once they're dry.

CRUISE CONTROL

CHAPTER FOUR

~ **M**alcolm ~

What gives a relationship a solid bond? If you ask that question to a random group of people, the answers you'd get would be common: attraction, sense of humor, and similarities in interests and hobbies would top the list. But there's another thing that can bond people just as much, if not more than all of those things. Sex.

Sex can be a bond as well, and when it gets its hooks in you, it can bond like the strongest super glue. It can fuse like welded metal, and once that happens, the only way to tear it apart is to grind it down to nothing and pry at it. Sex is an addictive drug, and it has me locked within its cages. I'm unable to free myself, but right now, I don't want my freedom. I hunger for imprisonment.

It's not common for me to say things like this, but Ava Pierson is my girlfriend. *Girlfriend*. Technically, we've been seeing each other for four months now, but it really just became official two months ago, when I removed her from my list of patients. I'm a relationship therapist, and yes, my girlfriend used to be my patient.

Now, I know what you're thinking. *Dr. Colson, how could you? That woman was your patient? Wow. You're a relationship therapist and you slept with a patient seeking therapy regarding a relationship? You're a pig, Dr. Colson.*

Maybe I am. I've never been one to care about the opinions of perfect strangers, so I'm unbothered by social stigmas or so-called taboo tropes that pull judgement from the lips of people who don't even know me. With Ava, the situation was different from my normal patient who's trying to maintain something she already has. Ava was an anomaly.

Ava came to me after a break-up with a man she'd been dating for a year. His name was Lucas Bay, and although I'd never met him, I took Ava on as a patient because the relationship had ended so recently, and she described the breakup more as an intermission. She led me to believe there was a good chance they would get back together, and that Lucas was still showing interest in her. It turned out that wasn't true. Ava only wished it was.

I'd be lying if I said my attraction to Ava didn't factor into my decision to take her on. If she'd come in with Lucas, I never would've thought to act on my attraction to her, but since she was by herself, my cock was like a devil on my shoulder, telling me to go for it. I tried to fight it throughout each session, but it only took four appointments with Ava before my barricades had been broken down and my cock was as deep in her as her pussy could handle.

The bond of sex has been locked in place ever since, and even after four months of seeing each other, I still crave her with every sight of her. My cock still twitches when she looks at me with her deep brown eyes, and licks her lips. I still fantasize about her when she texts me, telling me she wants me, and when we fuck, it's still the darkest, kinkiest version of heaven I can imagine.

My name is Dr. Malcom Colson, and I'm starting to think

I might need my own therapist. I've been a relationship therapist for over five years, and while I give advice to my patients with confidence and a deep understanding of what makes people tick, I'm not the best at taking my own advice. My girlfriend is my girlfriend for a very specific reason, and I've never been ashamed of my sex life. When it comes to sex, it's only good for me if I do it a specific way.

I'm a dom. If you don't know what a dom is, I assume you haven't read a book, been on the internet, or been to the movies recently. I crave dominance in sex. I ache for being the mastermind of pleasure and orgasmic bliss. I need to feel her quiver beneath my touch. I need to watch her body and her face change as I roam about her flesh. I need to learn what makes her tick, what gets her wet, and what makes her come. I need it this way, and Ava facilitates these desires better than anybody I've met in my thirty years of living.

It could be that growing up in Dover, Delaware made it to where my access to the world's kinkiest people was very limited. Dover is a small town, although it's surrounded by large cities that are all within three hours of my home. It's a quiet place, so maybe that's why finding women who are openly into BDSM and being submissive is hard to do. Or, it could be that Ava is just a special kind of woman whose desire to lose control happens to be the sexiest thing I've ever seen. She's sexy without even trying to be, lustful with no effort. She knows what I want and what I like, and she gives it to me without me having to ask for it. It's the perfect setup.

Our relationship is give and take. She gives me what I want, and I take that pussy the way she needs it taken. Both parties get what they want, and there's no confusion about who or what we are. As long as we're both satisfied, nobody has a reason to complain. Nothing can go wrong. Everything is perfect.

CHAPTER FIVE

~ **M**alcolm ~

"Happy birthday, dear Ava. Happy birthday to you."

The small gathering of waiters and waitresses finish up their song and begin to clap, as do a few tables next to us as Ava blows out a candle on her little cupcake and smiles for the audience. Once the staff of Outback Steakhouse disperses, Ava's smile fades in an instant.

"Ugh, I hate when they do that. It's so embarrassing, Malcolm," she says to me with both annoyance and delight in her voice. "Why'd you have to do that?"

"To embarrass you," I answer with a shrug. "I like seeing the look on your face when you're surprised."

"I bet you do," Ava shoots back with a sly grin, just before taking the candle out of the chocolate cupcake. She picks up the cake and takes a bite. I watch the chocolate frosting smear on her lips, and I have a quick flashback about the last time she had my cock in her mouth and cum smeared on her lips the same way. I feel a shiver run through me as I remember how she licked it away like it was the most delicious frosting. The woman sitting in front of me is a sexual force to be reckoned with.

After Ava wipes her mouth and puts the cake down, she sips her wine and looks at me with a smile. I smile back, although I know what both of us are thinking, and it doesn't involve smiles. Ava sips her wine before speaking to me over the glass.

"So, how was work? Anything new and exciting?"

"Well, first of all, you know I can't talk about my patients," I say, with a nod of my head. "Secondly, if you're wondering if I met a patient I'm attracted to the way I was attracted to you the first time you came gliding into my office, the answer is *of course not*. You don't have to keep asking me that."

"It's not that," Ava says with a playful smirk signaling her lie. "I just wanted to see how things were going at the office. I haven't been there in a while. Just interested in your work."

"I see," I say behind a scoff. "Well, it's going well. My list of patients keeps growing, so I'm busier than ever, but making great money while also helping a lot of people. Everything is running smoothly. Great patients, great money... you. Life is good."

Ava's body pauses while her eyes lock onto me. She's stunning tonight, wearing a red dress that hugs her body like a comforting friend. Ava is five-foot-six and a hundred-seventy pounds of pure thickness. In a dress like this, her ass and hips are on full display, and they draw countless eyes in her direction. Her dark brown hair is wavy tonight and flowing behind her shoulders, and her oval, brown eyes peer right into my soul. She's the most gorgeous woman in the room no matter which room she's standing in, and when she looks at me, I feel it in my chest.

"So, you're happy with me?" Ava asks as her eyes suddenly

fill with tears teasing to spill over. "You don't regret risking your career for me?"

I frown. "What? Of course not. The past couple of months have been great. I've got nothing to complain about, Ava. We're good."

Ava smiles so beautifully I swear I can hear the plates on the table let out a gasp. I know she has some insecurities that have carried over from her past and her relationship with Lucas. There are times when she needs reassurance, and I know it's all about problems with trust. The therapist in me knows Ava has issues she still has to deal with, but I'm no longer her therapist. I'm her boyfriend. My job isn't to provide therapy now, it's to support her, so while I know she has issues she's working on, I'm here for her now in a different capacity than before.

Before I can say anything else, Ava gets up from her seat. As she rises, she glares at me in the way she knows I love, and I stare back. I watch her straighten out her skin tight red dress, pulling the fabric down her thick, luscious body inch by inch, before finally walking over to my side of the booth and sitting down next to me.

Once she's seated, we both smile. I smile because I'm curious, she smiles because she knows what's coming. This is how we play with each other. This is why our sex is so unbelievable. This is what bonds us.

"You've been amazing, Malcolm," Ava says as she leans forward and places her face on her fist, leaning on it. "Our time together has been phenomenal for me, too. I really appreciate how good you are to me—how good you make me feel. I wanna make you feel good, too. Right now."

"What?"

Ava doesn't hesitate when she reaches down and grabs ahold of my thick cock beneath the table. She gasps when she touches it, as if she can feel how good it feels to me. I want to stop her, but when she starts to rub it, making it harder and harder, I'm the one who hesitates. I close my eyes for the slightest second, allowing myself a moment to sink beneath the waves of ecstasy, and the next sensation I feel is Ava sliding down my zipper.

My eyes shoot open, and I look down to find my bare erection in her hand. Ava has literally pulled my dick out under the table at Outback fucking Steakhouse.

"What the fuck are you doing?" I ask, my eyes darting around the restaurant to see if anyone has noticed what is happening. Luckily no one has yet, but that won't last forever. This dick demands attention.

"I want it, Malcolm," Ava whispers, leaning towards me. "I want to taste you all over my tongue. I want you so bad I can't fucking stand it. From how hard your cock is, I know you want me, too. So, if you don't take me out of here right now, I'm going to get on my knees under this table and make you come in the middle of my favorite restaurant. That's how bad I want it."

"Jesus Christ," I mutter, as Ava starts to stroke my cock vigorously.

It feels so good, and I know I should reach down and stop her, but I just don't do it. However, I can't let Ava get on her knees under this table. People will see her scooting her way down there. There will be no hiding it, so when a random waitress walks by holding a tray of empty plates, I reach out and stop her. "Excuse me. Can we get our check, please?"

The waitress can't see that my dick is in Ava's hand, but she can see her hand is under the table and moving around in my lap. She squints, before meeting my gaze again. All the while, Ava doesn't skip a beat. She keeps going as if the waitress isn't standing right next to us, and I know it won't be long before she decides to get on her knees. Ava won't care that the waitress is here.

I clear my throat and frown at the waitress, before reaching under the table to push Ava's hand to the side and reach for my wallet. I reveal two crisp hundred dollar bills, which should more than cover our steak dinners and multiple glasses of wine. I toss the bills on the table, shove my cock inside my pants, and fix my zipper. Ava flashes a quick, satisfied smile before sliding out of the booth, and leading me out the door, all while the waitress watches us with a bewildered look etched on her face.

alcolm ~

~M The inside of my truck is hotter than it should be, even with the heater set to seventy on this winter's night. As I drive away from the restaurant, I know there are people on the sidewalks. I know there are cars next to us as we sit at the stoplight, and every nerve in my body is aware of their presence. I can't help but think that they know what's about to happen inside this Chevy Silverado. They have to know. They have to see that Ava has removed her seatbelt and is leaning over the center console of the truck, unfastening my pants with both hands.

Ava's ass is pressed against the window—there's no way that ass isn't attracting attention—as she leans across the truck. I know I should stop this, because what if a cop rolled past us or pulled up next to us? What if someone started taking pictures to post on social media? People do that type of shit all the time. However, this is Ava, and this is us. I know she's going to get what she wants, because even though she's my submissive, until I command her, she will go for what she wants. Ava makes her own rules, until I come in and make her bend to my will.

"Ava," I mutter, but she doesn't even slow down, let alone stop. Let's be honest, I don't want her to anyway.

"I want it, Malcolm," she replies, completely focused on my zipper. She slides it down just as the light turns green, and by the time I'm done turning onto the highway, Ava has sucked the entire length of my cock into her mouth.

I let out a gasp, nearly slamming my foot on the gas and sending us hurling forward, but I manage to keep control of my feet. The warmth of her mouth feels so incredible as she slurps and sucks me. I try to focus on the road in front of me, but all I want to do is look over at her ass as it juts into the air like a luscious skyscraper. I reach over and grab it with my right hand, while my left controls the steering wheel, and Ava moans. The deep rumble of her moaning sends tiny vibrations into my cock, heightening the sensation.

"Goddamn," I whisper, fighting the desire to close my eyes and throw my head back.

Ava continues to suck me, moaning as her lips slide up and down my shaft. She loves it just as much as I do, which is just another reason I fuck with Ava like I do. She's not afraid to embrace her sexuality or the fact that she loves to give oral sex.

Women are often shamed for being sexual, especially when they enjoy giving pleasure just as much as they enjoy receiving it. It's bullshit. I'm a sexual man, and I fucking love having a pussy in my face. I love sticking my tongue into it and letting it glide over the clit. I enjoy giving pleasure, and no one would ever shame me for that—so why the hypocrisy when it comes to women? I love that Ava doesn't buy into that. Take what you want, baby. Do what the fuck you want to do.

I make another turn after a brief pause at a stoplight.

Luckily, there weren't any other cars there, so no one could see Ava's ass pressed against the passenger's window. I'm only a few minutes from home, and Ava has been sucking me nonstop. As much as I love it, I can no longer fight back the other side of me. The dominant side.

Knowing we're only minutes away from my housing development, I pull my hand away from Ava's ass and place it on her back. She thinks I'm encouraging her to keep going—to push me over the cliff of orgasm. However, the gesture is my signal for her to stop.

"Ava, stop," I command, my voice deep and controlling. "Stop. Now."

Hearing the seriousness in my voice, Ava slowly releases me. As she backs away, our eyes meet, and I can see the hunger in her. She craves me, but now it's time for something else.

I let my eyes roam Ava's body. She's so sexy it hurts. I love the look of her. I love watching her.

"Pull your dress up," I demand. My eyes dart back to the empty road before going back to Ava, who smiles, knowing I've taken control and yearning for what's next.

"Yes, sir," she says, breathing hard.

I hate that I have to take my eyes off of her to make sure I don't drive off the road, but the second I see we're safe, I look down at Ava's black panties. They're lace and decorative, and as much as I can appreciate that, all I really want is for them to be out of the way.

"Take them off," I say, before glancing at the road.

"Yes, sir."

Ava pulls her panties off, and my heart races at the sight of her tugging the lace over her heels and dropping the thin fabric onto the floor of the truck. Once the panties are discarded, Ava leans back in the large seat and looks at me, awaiting my next command.

I look at her for a second, enjoying the view and thinking about what I would do to her if I wasn't driving this truck. I wish I could touch her, but since I can't, I tell Ava what she's going to do next.

"Rub your clit for me," I tell her. "Rub it the way you'd want me to if I wasn't driving right now."

"Yes, sir."

Ava moves her hand slowly up her leg, dragging it out just to tease me. I smirk before licking my lips, as Ava's fingers find her clit and start to rub circles over it. She moans at her own gentle touch, and I feel the temperature in the vehicle skyrocket. It gets so hot that I have to turn down the heat, even though it's the middle of January and cold outside.

Ava starts to pick up speed, rubbing her pussy like she can't help herself anymore. She closes her eyes and bites her lip, which has always been something that turned me on. I don't know why, but there's something unbelievably seductive about a woman biting her lip. It sends me reeling every single time.

"Fuck, Ava. You're so fucking sexy," I tell her as she continues rubbing herself. "Look at me while you do it, and I want you to come for me. Let me see you come."

Ava's eyes pop over to me. "Yes, sir," she says, and when our eyes meet, I reach down and grab ahold of my stiff cock. Ava's eyes bounce back and forth between my eyes and my cock, and she rubs her pussy like she's in a room by herself. I know she likes watching me stroke myself, so I do it with vigor. I keep my eyes on the road, but I let my hand glide up and down my shaft as Ava watches me. I become her porn, and she becomes mine.

"Oh my god, I love watching you," Ava says behind labored breathing. Her breaths quicken, and I know she's getting close, so I stroke myself faster. "Oh fuck. Can I please fucking come?"

I hear her say it, but I can tell it's too late. She's too excited to hold it back now. I give her permission, but before I can finish saying, "Yes, you can come for me," Ava's skin is already flushed. She lets out a loud moan that makes my cock twitch in my hand, and I watch her come. It's my favorite thing in the entire world, even if I'm not bringing her to orgasm myself. Nothing excites me like her coming for me.

As Ava's orgasm relents, I turn the truck into my driveway. The garage door goes up as Ava's breathing finally starts to slow down, and I pull into the garage, closing it behind us. When I shut off the engine, Ava looks over at me and smiles. We're not done yet, and she knows it.

"So," Ava says, pausing to lick her lips. "What's next? Where do you want me, sir? Upstairs?"

I don't have to think of the answer. It's a no-brainer, and the thought of it tugs at the side of my mouth, making me smirk in anticipation.

"When you get inside, don't go upstairs," I say. "Go downstairs, and wait for me in the Black House."

CHAPTER SEVEN

Malcolm ~

I'm not afraid to admit who I am. I'm not normal. What is normal anyway? It's a subjective adjective that changes depending on the person using it. Normal for some people is vanilla sex—nothing but missionary and no oral or anal ever. Some people—lots of people, actually—have sex all the time and *never* orgasm. When I say people, I mean women. To far too many of them, that's normal. That shit will never be normal to me.

For me, normal is kinkery. With me, normal involves lots of spanking and multiple orgasms. It includes a plethora of toys designed to bring a woman to orgasm in a myriad of ways. Normal is pleasure masked as pain. Normal is bondage. Normal for me would scare the hell out of most people, and I like it that way. I don't want to be your version of normal, because I fucking *love* my version, and the Malcolm Colson edition of normal is showcased in the newest edition to my home. The Black House.

After Ava and I had been dating for about a month, I realized that the toys in my room just weren't enough. Don't get me wrong, I loved having Ava on her knees in front of my bed while I opened up the four drawers of pleasure beneath the bed frame. Nothing made me more excited than seeing the drawer full of floggers, or the one full of dildos, or the one full of vibrators. Those were my weapons of choice and I knew how to wield them. However, once Ava and I became a real thing, I knew it was time for an upgrade. Not only because Ava would appreciate it, but because I had grown as well. My desire to take control had grown from a seed to a beanstalk, and it was time to climb to the top.

The basement of my house was mostly empty before. I didn't have much of a need for it except to store some boxes here and there. Anything I couldn't find a specific space for upstairs found its way into the basement, where it collected dust until I remembered it was there and threw it out. Until I had an epiphany.

One morning, while browsing kink sites and looking for new toys to order, I realized I shouldn't stop with a new flogger with thick black braids. I decided I'd buy all new toys, but as I filled my kinky shopping cart with all-black whips and paddles, I realized I could buy an entire warehouse full of toys and put them all in my basement. I had a vision that hit me like a lucid wet dream, and before I knew it, I'd bought enough toys to turn my entire basement into a dark and twisted fantasy of pain and pleasure. I bought toys I'd never used before to go along with my all-time favorites, and even made a trip to Home Depot to purchase a new black door to the basement, and have black carpet installed. When it was all finished, I decided to call my new creation of fetish and desire the Black House. It fit perfectly, and I've never been more in love with a single room.

As I descend the stairs that I had painted black, I let my eyes take in the room as it comes into view. At the bottom, I step onto the soft black carpet and take it all in with a smile pulling at the corner of my mouth.

In the middle of the room is a black table topped with black, soft leather that matches the couch in the left corner of the space. The table has silver U hooks bolted to the long sides of it, which are designed specifically for rope or handcuffs to be fastened to them. The sight of the table alone makes me smile.

On the wall to the left is a black chest of drawers made of mahogany. I don't go over to it because I won't be using the toys in it tonight, but I know it's full of floggers of all sizes and thicknesses.

To the right of that is another chest of drawers that looks just like it, and it's filled with every dildo I could think of when I was searching online.

At the far end of the basement is a king size bed covered in black sheets with a black frame. The frame has four pillars reaching for the ceiling, and every pillar already has a black rope dangling down to the floor, waiting to be wrapped around my submissive's wrists and ankles.

Next to the wall on the right is a black sex swing, a black Sybian vibrator, and a new version of The Tremor floor vibrator, which I've only used once to amazing results. Next to that is a display of spreader bars in a glass case with a black frame, and a shelf of handcuffs.

The space is incredible, and everything in the basement is capped off by the giant toy to my immediate right. Just over my right shoulder, I see the outline of a black Saint Andrew's Cross that's taller than my six-foot frame. The cross resembles a massive X, and at each end of the arms are black cuffs. Out of everything I purchased for the Black House, this is my absolute favorite.

Just looking at it all makes my heart race. Everything in

me desires to use the toys in this room, and there isn't a better submissive for this lustful heaven than Ava.

When I look over my shoulder at Saint Andrew's Cross and find Ava kneeling in front of it, my cock grows from aroused to rock hard. She's completely naked with her hair tied into a tight ponytail that hangs behind her back. Her succulent curves command my attention as she waits for me with her head down but her confidence higher than ever.

"Are you ready, Ava?" I ask as I step towards her and begin to unfasten my pants.

"Yes, sir," Ava replies, just as I release my belt and let my pants drop to the floor.

"Good. Let's begin."

CHAPTER EIGHT

~ **M**alcolm ~

"You belong to me. Do you understand?"

"Yes, sir."

"You belong to me, but I do not own you," I explain as I stand Ava up and position her back against the Saint Andrew's Cross. I use my feet to spread her legs so they line up with the bottom legs on the large X. "Your body is mine to please, but you are still a free and powerful woman. You are a goddess. You're a queen, but you are giving yourself to me. Do you understand?"

"Yes, sir," Ava whispers, as I bend over and clasp the cuffs around her ankles.

"What is your safe word?"

"Cleopatra."

"Why?"

"Because I'm a queen."

"That's right. You're a queen, I'm a king, and tonight we're going to create our own world for us to rule together.

This basement is our kingdom, Ava. It's ours, to do with what we please. Are you ready?"

"Yes, sir."

Ava's breathing speeds up as I raise her hands above her head and place them on the upper arms of the X. The distinct click of the cuffs locking around her wrists pulls excitement from both of us, and once she is bound, I kiss Ava on the neck before taking a step back.

In front of me, Ava is locked into position with her limbs bound and spread. She's totally naked, and the sight of her standing there, waiting for me to dominate her, makes me harder than I can explain. My eyes roam about her exposed flesh, picking out the places I'm going to squeeze—the places that will tremble beneath my touch. Her tits call to me, and her bare pussy is the most inviting thing I've ever seen. I want to cover it with my mouth and look up at Ava's body as it shakes from the sensation of my tongue working its magic. All in due time.

Ava watches with anticipation as I walk away from her. I go over to the other side of the room where the chest of drawers are located and glance at them both. When I came down, I figured I wouldn't use anything in them tonight, but Ava's exquisite body has pulled me in a different direction.

I walk over to the first drawer and slide open the top. The first thing I see is the black flogger with thick black braids that started it all. It's the toy I was looking at when I decided to build this dungeon of pleasure. I lift it out of its place and smile at the feel of it in my hand. It has a weighted handle to offset the thickness of the braids, and once I'm holding it, I can't put it back down. I turn around and see Ava glaring at the flogger, her face struggling between anxiety and excitement, and I know I've made the right choice.

"Safe word?" I ask Ava for a second time, as I walk back

over and position myself in front of her. The new flogger dangles in my hand, poised and ready to be wielded.

"Cleopatra."

"Don't forget it," I say in nearly a growl, then I lift my hand and flick my wrist.

The braids of the flogger whip across Ava's breasts with a low but distinct crack and leave a slew of pink streaks on her flesh. Ava squeals, feeling both the sting of pain and bliss of pleasure. Her breathing quickens again, and I stand back to assess her reaction.

Is it too much for her? Is she going to use the safe word already? Being dominant to me doesn't mean being brutal. In fact, I'd say it means being even more sensitive to what she needs. There's an obvious line that can never be crossed, but it must be walked with careful precision.

I lower my head so my eyes are level with Ava's. We look at each other, and I wait for her reaction. I can tell she's shocked at the sensation of this particular flogger, but the shock doesn't look like discomfort. She looks turned on, and when Ava smiles at me, I know we're good. I flash a devilish smile of my own before flicking my wrist a second time, sending the braids streaking across Ava's breasts again. This time, the sound Ava releases isn't a squeal. It's a moan of unmitigated pleasure.

I use the flogger on Ava over and over again, spanking her hard enough to leave a mark, but soft enough not to hurt her too much. The braids crash on her chest, stomach, and legs, and Ava fills the basement up with the sound of her moaning and hard breathing.

After a few minutes, I stop to appreciate my work. Ava's body is covered in marks that have changed from pink to red, and both of us are exhausted. Breathing heavily, I step forward and place the handle of the flogger under Ava's chin to lift her head.

"You're such a good girl," I say, before licking my lips and pressing my mouth against hers. My tongue dances in Ava's mouth and hers follows my lead as I rub her sensitive body. I feel her breath shudder in my mouth when I run my hand over her nipples, and I know she's starting to feel delicate. Her body is ready for a change, and I'm ready to oblige, so I drop the flogger to the floor and lower myself to my knees. The second I'm down, I do what I've been dying to, and shove my tongue into Ava's pussy.

Ava lets out a loud gasp as I lick her clit over and over again. I'm like a machine, fighting through the fatigue I feel under my tongue from overuse. I caress Ava's clit and look up at her. Just because the room is black doesn't mean I don't want to see. I want to see everything. I love watching Ava close her eyes when the feeling becomes too much for her to keep them open. If you're not paying attention to your lover when you're in this position, you're setting yourself up for failure, because all the signs you need to tell you if you're doing it correctly are right there in front of you. It's all in her body language. Ava's body tells me I'm doing it right, and it hits a fever pitch when I slide two of my fingers inside her pussy and curl them upward to hit her g-spot.

"Oh, fuck!" Ava blares the second I touch the spot, and I use both my fingers and my tongue to bring Ava to a house-rattling orgasm. She earned it after being flogged.

I savor the taste of her in my mouth and relish the feeling of her wetness all over my face as I stand up.

"Taste it, Ava," I command, as I lean over and let Ava kiss me again. She licks all over my mouth and chin, sucking up her juices. This woman is so unbelievably hot. Every time she touches me I want to fuck her senseless.

I pull myself away from Ava once again, walking away from her without saying a word. She breathes hard behind me as I walk back over to the chest of drawers and place the flogger back inside. Once it's back in its place, I step over to the next chest of drawers and grab a black, cordless Magic Wand vibrator. It's smaller than the corded white ones, which is perfect for this occasion.

Before walking back to Ava, I make sure to remove my boxers. I know Ava is watching, so I take my time, standing there with my bare ass facing her, before sheathing my cock with a condom and turning around. Ava licks her lips when she sees my erect shaft, like she's literally hungry for it, and once we're face to face, I let her feel it just a bit by rubbing the head against her sensitive clit. She gasps for me, and I smile.

"Are you ready to feel every single inch of me?" I ask, just before leaning over and licking her neck.

She lets out a soft moan before answering, "Yes, sir."

I reach between us and grab ahold of my erection, pushing it inside of Ava with ease. She's so wet I'm surprised she isn't dripping, and I use the lubricant as motivation to go insane. I immediately start to pound in and out of Ava. Our bodies crash together repeatedly, and both of us moan into the air. I feel Ava wanting to reach down and grab me, but her hands and feet are still bound to the X, so she has no choice but to stand there and let me ravage her.

After a few minutes of pure fucking, I grip the vibrator in my palm and slide it between us, pressing it against Ava's clit. She lets out a shriek of surprise and pleasure as the vibrations start to work on her, and I know it won't be long before she erupts again. Fucking while standing up is a task, but I manage to pull it off with efficiency as I get up on the balls of my feet for extra leverage, and I'm spurred on by Ava's screams.

"Fucking Christ," Ava yells up at the ceiling. "I'm gonna come again. Oh, god! Can I please come? Shit!"

"Come for me..."

I'm interrupted by Ava's growling scream. She's rocked by an orgasm that seems as though it comes from the deepest parts of her soul, and the shriek she lets out is throat-shredding. The flesh on Ava's neck turns red and I see thick veins bulging just beneath her skin. Her orgasm is so fantastic, I couldn't hold back my own even if I wanted to. I let out my own howl of pleasure as I come with Ava, and both of us have nothing left to give except hard breathing and moans of exhaustion.

"Oh fuck," is all Ava manages to say as I pull myself out of her and drop the vibrator onto the floor. My body feels war-torn, and I want nothing more than to crawl over to the bed and go to sleep, but I take time to unfasten Ava from the cross. The second her limbs are free, both of us crash to the floor next to each other.

We breathe like we've just been saved from nearly drowning, and I don't even realize I've fallen asleep until I'm being woken up by a soft kiss on the cheek from Ava. When I open my eyes, she's fully dressed and back to normal.

"Goodnight, Malcolm. Sleep tight, my love," she whispers into my ear, just before stepping away and disappearing up the black stairs.

REPAIRS

CHAPTER NINE

Tessa ~

~ Monday mornings suck, even if you haven't just been dumped by your asshole ex-boyfriend. This particular Monday morning will be extra annoying, though, because today is the day I have to tell my mother that my relationship with Brandon is over. We all go through issues with our parents at some point or another, but my mother is on a whole different level, and this particular issue is in a completely different stratosphere for her.

My parents, Jack and Judy Milton, are traditional, to say the least. They're conservative by nature, and have a bad habit of pushing their agenda on me, even if I'm kicking and screaming the entire time. I love them, but we're almost nothing alike, and it causes tension.

For instance, my mother, Judy Milton, married my father when she was eighteen years old, and by the time she was twenty, I'd already been born. My father, Jack, was twenty-three on his wedding day. So, my parents have this notion in their head that I have to follow in their footsteps, while also wanting me to be more successful than them, even though they own their own business and are doing quite well for themselves. I'm proud of my parents' success, and that they met at an early age and have been able to stick together in a society where marriages end in divorce all the time. They're stronger than any couple I know, but when it comes to me, they've got it all wrong.

Milton Animal Clinic is owned by my father. He started this business when he was in his early thirties, after working for different veterinarians across Delaware. He's fifty-three now, so he's been running this business for a long time, and has made a good living. My mother has been right there beside him from the jump. She works at MAC as a groomer, but she's also a partner with my father on the business. I started working at MAC on my sixteenth birthday, and I'm still here twelve years later, assisting my father with whatever he needs at our little family business.

When I pull into the parking lot in my black Dodge pickup, I see the parking lot is missing a particular car. My closest friend is Melissa Backer. Missy for short, and I see that her red Infinity is missing from its usual spot in the corner. I don't know what she has going on today, but her not being here is only going to make talking to my parents about Brandon that much harder. She's usually a shoulder to cry on and a good buffer between me and my parents when things become too rocky in our work environment. Looks like I'll be facing the judgemental eyes of Jack and Judy alone.

The clinic isn't open yet, so I have to use my key to unlock the door, even though my mother is behind the counter watching me struggle. She stands there in a maroon blouse and her dark brown hair hovering just above her shoulders. Her face is stern and unmoving as if it was filled with Botox, although it isn't. I can tell from the particularly harsh glint in her eye that she's already heard about me and Brandon, and she's pissed.

"Thanks for the help, Mom," I say in lieu of a greeting once I manage to get past the locked door.

Judy brings her eyes up to meet mine without moving her head. "When I offer my help, you don't want to take it anyway. Why would today be any different?"

"Ugh," I spit back. "Is Dad in the back?"

"Not yet," my mother answers, her eyes going back to the computer screen in front of her. "He has an appointment in Dover this morning. It seems you and I have something to discuss on our own anyway, so I'm glad Jack isn't here right now. I received a phone call from Brandon this weekend, and he told me you broke it off with him. Kicked him out of your house, even."

What?" I nearly shout. The frown on my face is so tense it hurts.

"What has gotten into you, Tessa?" My mother goes on, ignoring my obvious confusion. "First, you stop coming to church with me and your father, and now you've broken up with a man you've been dating for two years. You seem to be making all these changes, and they're wrong. Tell me what has gotten into you."

Instead of walking to the back, where I work with my father, I place my bag on the counter in front of me and lean against it to talk to my mother.

"First of all, I didn't break up with Brandon, Mom," I announce. "He broke it off with me. It wasn't me making any changes. It was him, so maybe you should lecture him about making the wrong changes in his life."

My mother scoffs. "Well, if that's true, then you must've done something, Tessa. What could you possibly have done to make Brandon want to end things with you?"

"What? I didn't do anything."

"Oh please, of course you did. A man like Brandon wouldn't just act on a whim. You did something, and you need to confront it so you can find it in yourself to apologize and get him back."

"Get him back? He dumped me, Mom. He doesn't want to be with me, and I don't feel like fighting to get him back if he doesn't want me."

"Ava, when it comes to love, you have to let go of your selfishness," my mother scolds with a dismissive wave of her hand. "You can't sit around expecting everyone to cater to your desires and flights of fancy. Brandon is a good man, and you'll regret it if you end up missing out on him."

"Wow, Mom. Seriously? You sound just like him. I think I'll be fine. I've cried my last tears over Brandon."

"How can you be so naive?" Judy snips. "Brandon works hard, and is probably going to make himself a lot of money some day. You mean to tell me you don't want to be a part of that?"

"Mom, I want to be happy," I answer with pride, but it's dismissed with another wave.

"You need to be *secure*, Tessa. If all I cared about was my own happiness, me and your father never would've worked out. I had to sacrifice what I wanted so that we could be together. Now look at us. We have our business, and we make plenty of money. I'm happier now than I ever thought I wanted to be back then, and I just want the same for you.

"You're already twenty-eight, Tessa, and every year that passes, it becomes more and more difficult for someone your age to find a husband. You're running out of time. Please listen to me. I don't want you to end up alone."

If I frown any harder, I think my face will shatter. I knew she'd give me shit about losing Brandon, but I wasn't sure how bad it would be. Now that I know, I wish I would've called in sick again. Without Missy here to vent to, this is going to be the longest Monday in history.

"I don't even know what to say to that," I say, losing the

will to argue with her. "I don't know what you want from me. He dumped me because he wanted to go be with his band. He thinks he's going to make it big, and making it big requires being single, apparently. I would think you'd have my back on this. He dumped me. He dumped *your daughter*. It'd be nice if one day you could just be supportive, instead of trying to make me feel worse by placing all of the blame on me."

"I'm not your girlfriend, Tessa," Judy fires back without hesitation. "I'm your mother, and it's my job to be honest with you, and tell you how to navigate through life. I'm older and wiser than you. I know what's good for you, and I'm telling you if you don't go fight for Brandon, you're going to regret it when you see him on TV in a few years. He'll be out there spending his riches, and you'll be here with me, filled to the brim with heartache."

At this point, all I have the energy for is a disappointed shake of my head.

"I just want what's best for you, Tessa," Judy repeats. "Just think about it. Do you really want to end up alone? Are you really ready to sacrifice everything so that you can be *happy*? No relationship is perfect. They take work. You shouldn't just throw two years down the drain. Brandon might not be perfect, but he's going to be successful, and you could be right there on his arm when he's out and about, spending his millions on a brand new house for you to live in. Something tells me you'd be really *happy* then. Just get over yourself and think about it, Tessa. Don't mess this up."

With that, my mother turns on her heel and walks to the back of the clinic, leaving me at the counter with nothing but the tears I promised myself I wouldn't shed anymore.

CHAPTER TEN

~T~ essa ~

The therapist's office feels different this time. It's bigger without Brandon next to me. I don't feel trapped under the weight of his constant judgement, yet I feel more uncomfortable right now. Things haven't been the same, and I'd be lying if I said I wasn't affected by it all. If I wasn't affected, I probably wouldn't even continue these sessions, but here I am.

Dr. Malcolm Colson sits across from me with one leg crossed over the other. He's wearing light gray pants with a white button-up accented with gray buttons that match his pants. His shoes are white with gray strings that match the buttons. He's immaculate, and his green eyes look at me as if I'm the only person he has ever seen. He's focused, and even without saying a word, I feel like he cares. Dr. Colson is great at making me feel like I'm his only patient and therefore the most important, even though I know he's constantly taking on new clients. He's great at his job, and that's perfect because I need him to be at his best for me now.

"You're in your head a lot today," Dr. Colson says,

speaking first. Usually he opens with questions. Even the way we begin the session is different without Brandon.

After he speaks, he pauses to wait for a response from me. He's right, I am in my head right now, but I don't know where to begin. This week has been like being under the foot of a giant. All the weight is crushing me, and I can barely breathe. First Brandon, then my mother and all her judgmental shit, now I'm sitting in this room and realizing how different everything is without Brandon at my side. My world has flipped upside down. By the time I finish collecting my thoughts to actually speak to Dr. Colson, I have tears streaking down my face.

Dr. Colson slides over a box of tissue that he keeps on the table between us, and I quickly grab for one and grip it like a security blanket. After another silent pause for me to gather myself, Dr. Colson leans forward, drops his yellow pad on the table and speaks to me without breaking eye contact.

"It's okay, Tessa," he says in a hushed tone. "I can tell you've been through it since the last time we talked. Brandon obviously isn't here. There have been some changes, and that's fine. Things can happen fast like that. When you're ready, why don't you tell me what's going on. I'm here for you."

I swallow hard, because there's just something about trying to talk whenever you're emotional. The second you go to speak, tears just push their way forward like bouncers in a crowded club.

"Okay," I mutter, before taking a steadying breath. "I'm sorry for crying."

"Don't be," Dr. Colson interrupts. "We all have emotions, and you don't have to be sorry for displaying them."

"Thank you," I whisper before going on. "Things have just been crazy since the last time we spoke. Brandon isn't here because he broke up with me after our last session. Him and his stupid band went to a gig this past weekend, and we both said a bunch of things to each other, and it's really over. Then my stupid mom, who has no idea how to be supportive, did nothing but berate, criticize, and blame me for how things ended with Brandon. She made it seem like I was wrong for not chasing after him, and begging him to love me like some sad little puppy who can't be alone. She actually told me that the older I get, the less time I have for someone to marry me, as if that's what my whole life is dependent upon. As if the whole point of my existence is to be somebody's wife.

"She got married when she was really young, so she feels like I should do the same thing. It's so fucking annoying. I don't know why she can't see that I don't have to be like her, and that it's stupid to chase after a man who doesn't want to be with me. She acts like Brandon is her son, and I'm just some chick he was dating. She doesn't even care that he broke my heart. She acts like it's my fault. I just... I just fucking hate everything right now."

Dr. Colson waits for a moment, letting me get out everything I need to say before he chimes in.

"Is all of that true?" I go on without even knowing I wanted to. "Am I stupid for not fighting for Brandon? Do I have to be on the arm of a man at all fucking times? Is something wrong with me because I'm twenty-eight and single? Am I supposed to have been married with two kids by now?"

"Tessa, none of that is true," Dr. Colson answers the second I'm done talking. "First off, you're absolutely not stupid when it comes to Brandon. He ended it, and once one person in the relationship doesn't want to be a part of that relationship anymore, then it's over. That's the obvious part, but the most important part is knowing that you never have to chase anyone. If I'm being honest, Brandon made things much more difficult than they had to be. I don't know if he'll ever be as successful as he expects himself to be, but I do know that he didn't seem to appreciate you, Tessa, and that should be a minimum in a relationship. It's not asking too much to be appreciated and respected, regardless of what your career choices are, or even if you haven't figured that out yet. You don't have to be doing the same thing as your partner for them to acknowledge and be grateful for you. Brandon made it seem like being with you was his favor to you, when it's him who should've been thankful that you allowed him to be with you."

Dr. Colson sits back in his chair again and watches me for a second, but I don't have a response other than tears. I've never heard a man speak so sincerely about how a woman should be treated. Dr. Colson is amazing. I bet he's making some woman very happy.

"There's something I need you to understand, Tessa," Dr. Colson goes on as I dab my eyes with the tissue. "I don't mean to disrespect your mother, so please don't take this that way, but you don't ever need a man to validate you. You don't need *anybody* for that. The only person you need to validate you is you. You're incredible as long as *you* believe you are. It doesn't matter what I say, or what your mother says, or what your father says, or what Brandon says. You're not supposed to dedicate your life to being some guy's arm candy. You are much more than that, and anybody who doesn't see that, isn't worth your time. You're a queen. You have to always remember that, because half the guys who are running around believing they are kings, are the court jesters of the world. They're just too dumb and full of themselves to realize it.

"You are a powerful woman, and you don't need anybody to substantiate you. All you need, Tessa, is to figure out what you want, and to go for it. You don't have to follow someone else's rules. So, forget about Brandon. Forget about your mother. The only person you have to please is you. The only person you have to impress is you. The only person who can legitimize you is you. The only person you have to answer to is yourself. You just need to go for what you want."

"What if I don't know what I want?" I ask. The tears have finally dried up, and I hope with everything in me that I'm able to keep them at bay from now on. "I've gone my entire life doing what other people have told me I needed to do in order to be loved, and the end result has always been heartbreak and dissatisfaction. I don't even know what I like. I'm twenty-eight years old. How am I supposed to fix that now?"

"It's never too late to get started," Dr. Colson says with a smile. "Maybe it's time you get to know yourself. Figure out what makes you happy, what you like and don't like, and what you want out of life. Once you do that, it'll be a lot easier to figure out what you want out of a relationship."

I let out a soft chuckle. "That sounds a lot easier said than done."

"It definitely is, but it's possible. There's no rush when it comes to learning about yourself. You go at your own pace."

"Okay. Is that something you can help me with? I'm just not sure I can do it on my own right now. It's kind of a foreign concept for me."

Dr. Colson smiles again, his face shifting into something sneakier than normal, before softening and looking more familiar.

"I absolutely can help you with that," he says, his voice overflowing with confidence.

I don't know what this alternate version of myself would look like. I've always given consideration to what my mother might think before I did anything. If it wasn't her, it was my father. If not him, it was Brandon for the last two years. I've never stopped to ask myself what it is I want. What do *I* like? What makes *me* happy? Now that the idea has been planted in my head, I'm dying to know the answers.

CHAPTER ELEVEN

~ T essa ~

"I can't believe you left me at that place to fend for myself."

"I'm sorry," my friend Melissa screeches, throwing her hands over her face. "What did you want me to do? Emma is sick and throwing up, and Daniel had to go to work. I'm so sorry, Tessa. I'm sorry I took care of my sick daughter. Next time, I'll leave her to fend for herself so I can be there for you in your time of need. After all, Emma is four now. She should be able to take care of herself like a big girl. I shouldn't spoil her like I did when she was three."

Both of us break into giggles, and I have to put my hand over my mouth to keep from spitting out the swig of vodka cranberry I just sipped.

"Oh shut up," I manage to say after I swallow. "I know you had to stay home because that child care center on the Air Force base will give you shit if you send your sick kid there, but now I'm giving you shit for making me face Judy alone. It's like she knew you weren't there, so she went extra hard on me. Next time, Danny is the one who has to stay home."

"Okay, I'll tell him," Melissa says behind a giggle. Daniel works on Dover Air Force Base as a civilian engineer, while Melissa works with me at Milton Animal Clinic. So, if one of them has to stay home from work, it's going to be Missy.

Melissa Backer has become my absolute best friend over the past eight years when she started working at my father's clinic. She's only a year older than me, and her sense of humor is off the charts. Missy is just the kind of person who always seems to have it figured out. She married Daniel when she was only nineteen years old, and while a normal person would've freaked out about being pregnant at the age of nineteen, Melissa gathered her thoughts and figured out how to make it work. She married her high school sweetheart, got an Associate's degree, and settled down in a life I could only dream of. Now she's twenty-nine with two kids, has been married for a decade, and seems genuinely happy with her life—minus a few sexual miscues from Danny every now and then, but there's no surprise there.

Missy and I hit it off from the day she walked into MAC, and we haven't slowed down since. I know all about what she goes through at home with Danny and the kids, and she knows everything about my life of drama with boyfriends and parents. She's my secret-keeper, and I'm hers. I love her to death, because her presence always makes things easier. She lightens the mood, no matter how dark the room may be, and after a long day of my bitching mother and going to therapy, I was beyond excited when she agreed to meet me at the bar in Applebee's for a drink to blow off some steam. Missy is my relief valve.

"All right, kid. Tell me what happened with Judy," Missy says, as she reaches for her sweating glass of Red Bull and vodka.

"Okay, so remember how I told you what went down between Brandon and me?" I begin. I turn my body in the seat to face my beautiful redheaded friend, whose hair is loose and cascading down her back like a bloody waterfall. "Well, when I got to work, expecting to have to explain everything to Judy myself, she comes at me the second I get through the door. Apparently, Brandon called her and told her everything. He even tried to make me the asshole by saying I kicked him out of my house. Of course, my mother believed what he said and got mad at me like Brandon is her favorite child. She told me I was running out of time to get married because I'm twenty-eight."

"Ooh, the fucking audacity!" Missy barks.

"Right! She's horrible with that shit. God, I just feel so stressed out right now."

"Maybe you should go talk to that gorgeous therapist of yours."

"First of all, I did go see him today," I explain. "Second of all, don't even start."

"What? It's not my fault he's gorgeous," Missy says behind a giggle. "I remember after we looked him up online, then I saw him leaving his office downtown one day. I was like, 'Well hello Mr. Therapist! I think I'm due for some one-on-one time. How about we go back in there and close the door. Maybe we lay down on the couch. Maybe you show me your therapeutic cock and balls!'"

"Oh my god, Missy."

"Shove those beautiful balls right in my face."

"Missy!" I bellow, before diving into a laughing fit. "Something tells me Danny would have a problem with that."

"You think?" Missy laughs again. "You know I love my Danny, but something tells *me* Danny isn't packing what your therapist has dangling between his legs. That man is a god. Don't worry, Tessa, you know I'd never lay a finger on anyone other than Danny... and myself. A girl needs orgasms, after all."

Both of us laugh together again, and all the weight I felt on my shoulders before I made it to the bar feels like it has been lifted off. It probably has something to do with the tiny buzz I'm feeling now, but Missy is the biggest culprit. She just knows how to clear the clouds on a rainy day.

"So, can I ask what Mr. Sexy Ass said in therapy, or is that just between the two of you?" Missy asks as she adjusts the shoulder straps on her blue dress.

"Well, I don't like to really get into it, but he does such a good job of telling me what I need to hear. I think he's a super feminist or something, because he makes me feel empowered. Basically, he told me I don't need anyone to validate me. He said I'm a queen."

"Wait!" Missy puts a finger in the air. "That beautiful man told you you're a queen, and you managed to *not* ride him like a rollercoaster right there in the office? You're literally the strongest woman I know."

We both laugh. "I'm not going to try to fuck my therapist, Missy."

"Why not?"

"Because he's my *therapist!*"

"Therapists still fuck! *Especially* this therapist. He's a *sex* therapist for cryin' out loud! I bet he'd fucking tear a girl from limb to limb with that dick. Ugh. I can only imagine."

"He's a relationship therapist first, sex therapist second, and why are you fantasizing about my therapist?"

"Because I can. Fantasizing isn't cheating. I know I'm married, but you, on the other hand, can do whatever you want now that you're finally free of the world's most annoying and talentless music producer. Or is it manager? Who fuckin' cares. Anyway, you should be going crazy now."

I release a loud sigh. "Yeah, I know. You're probably right, but I'm hesitant. Anytime I was single in the past, my mother was always in my ear about how I needed to meet someone. She made me feel like being single and having fun made me a whore, and when I met Brandon she was so thrilled. Now that I'm single again, I don't know how I want to do it. I know Judy will be in my ear nonstop, reminding me over and over again that I can't be out there doing whatever with whoever, but I just feel different this time."

"Good," Missy chirps. "You *should* feel different, Tessa. You're a grown woman. You can literally do whatever you want."

"I know that's true, but it's more complicated than that," I try to explain, but even when I say it, I'm not sure I understand or believe it.

"It doesn't have to be, sweetie," Missy says. "At the end of the day, it's your life, not Judy's or Jack's."

Missy is right, just like Dr. Colson. It is my life and I can do what I want, and no matter how much thought I put into it, I can't shake this feeling that there's something on me that I need to get off—some extra weight I need to put down so I can be free. I just don't know what it is or how to get rid of it.

"Umm, excuse me."

Our conversation is interrupted by a deep voice coming from behind me. Before I even turn around, I see the expression on Missy's face. She looks shocked, so when I start to turn around, I don't know what to expect. Is it Brandon coming to try to get me back?

When I lock eyes with the man standing next to the empty seat beside me, I quickly realize it is *not* Brandon. Brandon couldn't look like this on his best day.

"Hi," the man says, with a seductive smile accented by a five o'clock shadow. "Is this seat taken?"

CHAPTER TWELVE

~ **T**essa ~

    "Umm," I mutter, as I stare at a beautiful man with dark brown, and wavy hair. He's at least six-one, with a thin frame and blue eyes. His lips are thin and he has a strong jaw paired with broad shoulders. For some reason, he's wearing a suit in Applebee's, but he makes it look so good I don't even focus on why anyone would be here in a suit. Hands down, he's the most handsome man in the restaurant, and it's not even close.

"This seat right here," he says with a smile that nearly knocks me from my seat. "Is it taken?"

"Uhh, no, it's not," I manage to force out. "It's all yours."

"Thanks," he says, and while my eyes are still bulging, I turn around to look at Missy, who mouths the words, "Oh my god."

"So, what's your drink?" the man says, pulling my attention back to him. "Is that a vodka cranberry?"

"Mm-hmm," I answer between pinched lips.

"Can I get you another one?"

"Uhh..." I look over at Missy, who takes this opportunity to speak for me.

"Yes, you can. She'd *love* another drink," Missy blurts, smiling like the Cheshire Cat.

"Great," the unnamed man says, before waving to the bartender. "Hi. Let me get a Jack Daniel's on the rocks, and a vodka cranberry, please." The bartender steps away to make the drinks and returns to set them in front of my new companion. "Thank you. Here you go," he says, sliding my new drink over to me, even though I haven't finished my first one yet.

"Thank you," I say.

"You're welcome. I didn't mean to interrupt your conversation, so I just wanted to make amends with a new drink. Enjoy," he says, then he sits straight and focuses his attention on his drink and whatever is going through his mind.

I'm not sure what to say, so I don't respond at all. Instead, I turn to face Missy and find that she looks furious.

"What are you doing?" she whispers.

"What?"

"Talk to him," Missy whisper-screams, and I frown, hoping she'll recognize my face as a signal to keep her embarrassing voice down. "Brandon couldn't look that good if he traded faces with Jesus. You see my goofy face all the time, so quit bullshitting and talk to him."

"Ugh. I'm not good at that kind of stuff, Missy."

"Oh my god, just fucking do it, Tessa. Just be yourself and you can't go wrong," Missy fires back, just before lifting herself out of her chair and walking away. "I'm going to the bathroom."

"Oh, I hate you," I say as she strides away with her nose high in the air, ignoring me. "*Hate*! I *hate* you!" I say again, accidentally grabbing some attention from the closest table, which I ignore.

Admittedly, I've been hit on plenty in my life. Even when I was with Brandon, guys would always try to come talk to me, and Brandon would get all insecure and we'd end up fighting about it as if it was somehow my fault.

I don't hit on guys, though. So, this thing Missy wants me to do is new to me, and even though the guy next to me is extremely attractive, I struggle to find the words. I have to think about it, and decide to take Missy's advice and be myself.

I clear my throat. "Well, I can't let you buy me a drink without at least learning your name."

Oh god. Was that stupid? Did that sound stupid? Shit, do I have something in my teeth? I know I haven't eaten anything from the menu, but maybe something got in there anyway. Cranberries? Are there any cranberry chunks at the bottom of my glass that could get stuck in my teeth? Shit.

"Liam," the man says, cutting off my thoughts, which I should thank him for. "Liam Gardner. And you are?"

"Tessa Milton," I answer, and the two of us shake hands. His is twice the size of mine and wraps around my dainty little hand like a warm blanket.

"It's nice to meet you, Tessa," Liam says with a megawatt smile. "You here blowing off steam, too?"

"Yeah, I most definitely am," I tell him with a half-hearted smile of my own.

"Yeah, me too. You know, when you're born, they should print out a memo that tells you how annoying your parents will be when you get older so you can be prepared."

I giggle. "Right? Yeah, that would be helpful. I wish someone would've told me how crazy my mother would be. Probably could've saved me years of therapy."

"I hear you. Cheers to that," Liam says, raising his glass and tilting it towards me for a toast. I have to react fast and raise my glass to meet his. "My father is a lawyer, and

I'm a paralegal. I'm sure you can imagine how disappointed he is."

"Ah, I see. Dad wants you to take the bar and be like him," I state.

"Exactly, and no matter how good I am at my job, it's never good enough for him. Even if he wins case after case because of my legal work, it means nothing. I'll never be good enough until I'm doing what he's doing. To him, I'm nothing if I don't take the bar exam. He's getting ready to retire and wants me to take over his firm. Maybe I'd want to do it if he wasn't so pushy about it, you know? But if I chose to do it, I'd want it to be on my terms. I'm done doing shit because he wants me to. At some point, parents have to realize that their kids have lives of their own, and at some point, kids have to say, 'Fuck what my parents think.' You know?"

As surprised as I am about how Liam, a complete stranger, just opened up to me about his personal business, I can't help but relate. If only I'd been given a manual on how to deal with my mother and her expectations, maybe I wouldn't feel like such a disappointment to her all the time. If only life was that easy.

"Unfortunately, I know *exactly* what you mean," I say to Liam as I finish off my first drink and slide the one he bought in front of me. "I'm having to deal with my mother in the same way right now, that's what I'm drinking to. I guess I never got to the point in my life where I could tell my parents, 'Fuck you.' I think, maybe, I'm finally getting there."

"Better late than never," Liam says. "The hardest part of it for me is accepting that making my own decisions and living my life the way I want is something I have to do for me. I also have to learn to be okay with pissing my father off. As kids, we never want to disappoint our parents, but when you're an adult and miserable because you're still trying not to disappoint them, that's when you know it's time for a change. It's hard, but we have to accept that they don't have to like what we do, they just have to respect us, and if they can't respect us for making our own decisions, it's okay to love them from a distance. In my case, loving him from a distance just might be my only option."

Liam knocks back the rest of his drink and places the glass back on the soaked napkin with a thud. I can tell that whatever he has been through has him emotional, and he just wanted to blunt the pain with a quick drink. Unfortunately, he doesn't have a Missy to clear his cloudy skies.

"Well, I've rambled to a stranger enough for one night," Liam says as he stands up and drops a few dollars on the counter to tip the bartender. "It was nice talking to you, Tessa Milton. Thanks for letting me vent."

"It was nice talking to you as well," I reply, doing my best to smile through the emotion our conversation conjured up. "I hope everything works out for you."

"Thanks. I think it will," Liam states. He stands up straight and smiles. "I don't know the ins and outs of your situation with your mother, but it sounds sort of similar to mine. Don't forget that it's your life. She doesn't have to like what you do, but she should still respect you. If she can't, you'll know what you have to do. Your happiness is always the most important thing. Have a good night, Tessa. Hopefully, I'll see you here again some time."

"I hope so. That'd be nice," I reply, just before Liam turns on his heel and walks out of the restaurant.

Once Liam is gone, my mind starts to run wild with thoughts. Between my therapy session with Dr. Colson, and now my conversations with Missy and Liam, I feel more motivated than ever. Maybe Brandon dumping me wasn't such a bad thing after all. Maybe it's the start of an important part of my life. The way I'm feeling right now, the next steps in my life might not be anything my mother can appreciate.

But, maybe that's okay. My happiness is the most important thing.

"So, how'd it go?" Missy asks from behind me as she reaches her seat and sits back down. "I may have watched you two from across the room. So, did you get his number? You guys having sex later on tonight?"

"Geez, Missy. You're wild tonight," I say behind a giggle and another swig of my drink from Liam.

"Well, you're single now, and I'm trying to live vicariously through you. So, spill the beans before I have to go home to my husband."

"Well, don't judge me, but I didn't get his number." Missy lets out an exaggerated sigh. "Leave me alone. He just got up and left, there was nothing I could do. He just said he hoped he'd see me here again sometime, and that's fine because I don't think I'd want this number right now anyway."

"What? What's *wrong* with you? Why not, Tessa?"

"Because I think I need to just take some time to myself," I reply, sipping my drink again. "I think I want to take some time to enjoy being single. Maybe I'll give you a reason to live vicariously through me."

"I'm confused."

"That guy is the type you settle down with. He's the guy you commit to, and I have no intention of settling down or committing to anyone right now."

Missy bulges her eyes at me before releasing an ear-to-ear smile.

"Oh okay! I see you, Tessa. I'll drink to that. Your mom is going to be salty, though."

Now it's me who smiles from ear to ear. "Yeah. I know."

CHECK ENGINE LIGHT

CHAPTER THIRTEEN

~M alcolm ~

"Wow, there's a lot of people here."

"Yeah, *too* many," I reply, just as my shoulder is bumped by a teenager holding hands with a girl who looks entirely too young to be allowed in the mall without her parents, let alone walking hand in hand with another kid too young to be alone.

"Aww, it's okay," Ava coos, as if consoling a baby. She reaches up and grabs a hold of my face, squeezing my cheeks as she wiggles my face side to side. "Poor baby. Don't worry. We'll be seated in the theater before you know it."

I smile and nod along, but on the inside, I'm fuming. Growing up in my parents' house wasn't some horrible ordeal that ruined my entire childhood, but it did have its issues. One of those issues was how violent my mother could become at a moment's notice. She could go from loving to choking you in zero seconds flat. She always felt she had to overdo things because I was a growing boy, and the bigger I became, the more she felt she needed to keep me in check by upping the violence. To her, my size and the fact that I'm a man was enough of a threat to her to make her lash out and overcompensate for our size difference. She was a short woman, the moment she started having to look up at me, she changed.

I loved my mother, but my face is off limits because of her. Being punched in the face while wearing braces can leave a permanent scar on the inside of you. My mother died two years ago, but the damage she caused will never be laid to rest. When Ava touches my face, it literally rubs me the wrong way, and I pull away.

"Oh, come on, grumpy pants. Let's go." Ava ignores my obvious annoyance, and begins walking towards the movie theater.

In Dover, there is only one movie theater, and it's inside the mall. I really hate it, but I love going to the movies, so I'm stuck between a rock and a bunch of annoying teenagers. After crossing the food court and pushing through the fog of intermixed smells of different foods, we finally make it to the theater. There's a line outside the ticket booth, and the two of us find our way to the back of it.

"Stupid lines," Ava says with a shrug. "I'm glad we came early enough. I can't wait to see this. How about you?"

Ava turns to me and wraps her arms around my waist. It's a show of affection that's aberrant, because we don't usually do things like that. We're dating, officially, but our relationship isn't one of public displays of affection. We don't do a lot of kissing or hand holding because it's just not our thing. We fuck. That's what I'm used to. Kisses and warm embraces aren't usually part of the equation.

I'm fine with us withholding the PDA. With Ava, I don't feel an urge to be overly affectionate. I know what we do, I remember how we met, and I know both of us well enough to know we're not in love. Ava and I are far from a rom-com, so when she wraps her arms around my waist, it's the second time I've felt uncomfortable since we walked into the mall.

"Umm, yeah," I mutter. "It's gonna be a good one."

"What's the matter with you today? You seem stressed. Work getting to you? You could always quit, you know? You don't have to spend all your time talking to women about their relationships."

"What?" I frown, because this isn't the first time Ava has mentioned my job as if she has a problem with it.

I know what it's about. I met her in my office, and the two of us ended up where we are now, so Ava thinks if it happened for her, it could happen for someone else. She's paranoid, and the thought of it stays in her mind so much, she can't help but keep mentioning my job.

"I mean, I know you love your job," Ava says. I can see the wheels turning in her head, trying to find a way to explain her comment. "I'm just saying, maybe it's stressing you out. It's a lot to have to deal with so many women's problems."

"Why do you keep saying women?" I snip, trying not to talk too loudly. "I'm a relationship therapist, Ava. I get just as many men in my office as I do women."

"Oh, yeah I know," Ava tries to backtrack, just as the line moves up. "Oh, look we're next."

Ava and I approach the counter and order our tickets, although I'm feeling surprisingly annoyed by how this evening has started. I nod to the woman who hands the tickets to me after I pay, and she smiles harmlessly as we walk away.

Once we're out of earshot of the booth, Ava turns around and glares at the woman. I notice her walking forward but looking backwards, so I turn around to find the woman staring at Ava with a bewildered look on her face. The two of them seem to be having a staring contest, but I'm guessing only one of them knows why.

"What's up? You good?" I ask, and before Ava answers,

she takes my hand in hers and pulls me closer to her, while still staring at the woman in the booth.

"I'm *fine*," Ava replies, as she finally turns around with a boastful look on her face. "Let's get some popcorn."

"Umm, cool."

The two of us walk to the concession stand, where we have to wait in another line. While we wait, Ava still has ahold of my hand. I catch her stealing glances back at the ticket booth, but the woman inside is busy with other customers. Ava doesn't seem to care, and stares daggers at the booth even when the woman isn't looking. After a few customers order candy and sodas, it's our turn to step up.

The woman behind the counter is more teenager than woman. She looks like she's probably seventeen, maybe eighteen at best. Definitely a teenager, and definitely not a threat. However, it doesn't matter to Ava.

The moment we step up to the counter, Ava looks tense. Her face is tight, and she is now directing the glare she was giving to the ticket booth at the young blonde in front of us.

"Hi. What can I get for you?" the worker says, her blue eyes peering up at me.

"Hi, let me get a large popcorn with extra butter," I tell her. I choose to ignore the way Ava is gawking at the kid. "Let me get some Twizzlers, too. Ava, do you want something to drink?"

My eyes turn to Ava, who is still staring at the concession worker. The blonde notices, and now stares at Ava with a frustrated look on her face. It doesn't matter if you even know why it's happening—no one likes to be stared at, so I'm not surprised when the teenager behind the counter shows some attitude.

"Ava," I say again, but it's too late to stop whatever has started.

"Uhh, yeah, I know exactly what I want," Ava finally says,

but from the tone and volume of her voice, I know what she wants has nothing to do with movie theater snacks. "What I *want*, is for this fucking cunt to stop staring at my man like she's ready to drop down and suck some dick right here at the concession stand. *That's* what I fucking want, bitch!"

CHAPTER FOURTEEN

~ **M**alcolm ~

"What the fuck?" the blonde teenager replies, her face twisting into a shocked scowl of surprise and fury.

"Don't play dumb, bitch. I see you," Ava barks, drawing the attention of every single person in the room now. All eyes are on us. "I'm standing right here in front of you, and you're going to stare at my man like I don't even exist. I will fucking beat the shit out of you right here in front of everybody."

"What are you talking about?" the concession worker shouts. I can tell she doesn't want the drama, but when someone brings it to you with such aggression and volume, it's hard to stay composed.

"I saw you, you dumb bitch," Ava shouts again. Ava's skin is turning red as she literally heats up like a bomb exploding in slow motion.

"You didn't see me do anything, you psycho," the worker responds, just as the manager on shift comes out of the back with her hands up, wondering what the hell is going on.

"Umm, what's the problem?" the young black woman says. By now, the entire room is wondering the same thing, including me.

"Oh, you wanna get involved in this?" Ava bellows, pointing at the manager. "This dumb bitch is hitting on my man, and if you're about to come out here and defend her, then me and you will have a problem, too."

"Ava, what the fuck are you doing?" I ask, but when I see Ava's face, I can tell she's seeing red. She has a scowl I've never seen on her before. I barely even recognize her.

"Miss, if you could just calm down, and maybe not make a scene," the manager pleads in a peaceful tone. "It seems to be just a misunderstanding. I'll even comp you your popcorn for free. Let's just not escalate things unnecessarily, please."

"Don't tell *me* to calm down!" Ava screams, slamming her fist on the counter. "I don't want your fucking popcorn. I want this bitch to be more respectful, because I swear to God, I will burn this whole building to the ground over my man. You hear me, you whore? I wouldn't care if I had to burn it down with both of us still inside so he could get away from you, I'd do it. I'd kill us both before I let you have him."

Everybody within earshot lets out an audible gasp, and I'm suddenly reminded of some of the things I learned about Ava when she was my patient. I remember the shock I felt when she told me her ex-boyfriend's porch had been set on fire. She claimed she didn't do it, but it was obvious to me that she had. Her ex ended up moving away because of how intense Ava's fixation on him had become.

"Ava, what the fuck?" I growl, razors in each word. "You can't say shit like that."

"Miss, I'm afraid I'm going to have to call the police," the manager says, just as she places a hand on the shoulder of the blonde concession worker, pulling her away from the counter like a protective mother. "This is getting out of hand, and you've made a direct threat against the building. I think we'll just let the police handle this."

"No, please. You don't have to do that," I plead, although I know the manager is exactly right. If I were in her position, I would call the police, too. Since I'm Ava's companion, however, I feel the need to try to defuse the situation. "We're going to leave. It's okay, we're leaving."

Luckily, my words seem to give the manager pause, as she stops at the door she came out of and waits. She looks at me before glaring at Ava, who's standing at the counter glaring at both of them like she's really ready to set something ablaze. If she had matches with her, the fire department would be on its way right now.

"Fuck that, I'm not going anywhere," Ava blurts. "Fuck both of you. He is *mine*!"

"Goddamnit, Ava, nobody cares. This isn't even about that. Let's just go before you get arrested over this stupid shit."

I reach out to grab Ava's hand, but she snatches it away. I try it a second time, and I'm able to grip her wrist and pull her gently towards the door. Reluctantly, and while maintaining her intimidating gaze at the workers, Ava lets me guide her out of the theater.

We walk quickly through the food court, avoiding the staring, judgmental gaze of everybody who was able to hear Ava's outburst, and push through the exit. It was only a few minutes, but the whole ordeal felt like it lasted an hour before I was able to pull her away. Once we're outside, I stop and turn to her.

"What the hell was that?" I bark, while still trying to keep my voice down. "That kid was a teenager, and she wasn't doing anything wrong. She was just taking my order, Ava."

"Maybe you didn't see it, Malcolm, but she wanted you. I saw it in her eyes," Ava says, and I can tell she really believes it. There was no evidence to support this claim, but in Ava's mind, the concession worker's eyes were enough to cause the whole scene, and there isn't a single bone in her body that regrets it.

"Well, nobody else saw it, Ava. All they saw was you, a grown woman, harassing a teenager. You can't do shit like that. It's unnecessary and embarrassing."

"I wasn't trying to embarrass you, Malcolm. I would never do that," Ava says. She steps closer to me, and I feel an urge in my stomach to take a step back, but I don't. "I only did it because I felt the need to defend you. I felt threatened, and you know I've dealt with bullshit in the past. I just wanted to make sure she knew that you're mine. You're *mine*, and I'm yours. That's it. I don't care how crazy I look to people who don't know anything about us. We belong to each other. Right?"

Ava looks me in the eyes, and I know she needs me to agree with her. Knowing her history the way I do, if I say the wrong thing here, it might have catastrophic effects. With that thought, though, I realize just how volatile this situation is. Ava is the embodiment of kinky perfection in bed and the Black House, but is all of that worth it *outside* the bedroom?

I swallow hard as Ava takes another step forward and grabs both of my hands. She holds them there, looking up at me, awaiting my response. I don't know what to say, because I'm conflicted. I know what she wants to hear, but I also know how I feel right now.

"We need to go," I say, after too long of a pause. "We need to get out of here before the cops actually show up. I don't want to stand here watching you get hauled off to jail."

Ava doesn't look happy, but she nods her head.

"Yes, sir," she says, before unveiling a seductive smile.

I know what she's trying to do, and it takes everything in me to ignore it and guide us to my truck. As we exit the parking lot, we drive right past a cop car with its lights on, and I watch in my rearview mirror as the car drives up to the doors we just exited.

CHAPTER FIFTEEN

~ **M**alcolm ~

"Good morning, Keisha."

"Good morning, Dr. Colson," my assistant, Keisha, says as I walk past her. I rub my temples, doing my best to reduce the headache that's been bombarding me since yesterday. "You okay? You look beat down."

"I'm all right," I lie. "Long day yesterday. I'll be fine. Who's first today?"

"Tessa Milton in half an hour," Keisha reminds me. "You need some Excedrin? My husband swears by it. He always gets migraines, and it's the only over-the-counter medicine that works for him."

"Yeah, Excedrin is great. I took two before I even left the house. Hopefully it'll kick in before Tessa gets here. Anyway, talk to you soon."

"Have a good day, Dr. Colson," Keisha says with her signature, comforting smile. "Feel better."

I step into my office and let the door close behind me. I feel the weight of an entire solar system pressing down on me this morning, and it all stems from the theater incident yesterday.

Ava and I don't go out on dates often. In fact, it happens so rarely, everything about yesterday felt awkward. Although Ava and I have been dating for a couple of months since I discharged her, we've never been able to connect on a friend-ship level. Everything with us has been sexual. It's sex all the time, almost daily, but that part of it never gets old, which is why I don't understand why we can't move into something more serious.

I shouldn't be surprised by any of this. I knew what I was getting when I signed up for Ava. It isn't a surprise to me that it's all about sex, and it's no surprise to me that I enjoy that side of our relationship so much. I am who I am, and I need a certain type of dominance when I fuck, and make no I mistake about it—I love to fuck. Not everybody can handle someone like me in the bedroom, so that makes Ava special in a sense. The sex we have makes what other people do look like fucking amatuer hour.

Most men would crumble beneath the pressure of trying to satisfy Ava's appetite for sex. It's part of the reason things didn't work out between her and Lucas. She wanted more in the bedroom, and he wasn't capable of providing it. She was too much for him, but it wasn't just in the bedroom. Ava was too much for Lucas all around, so he had to run away just to escape the breathtaking fog that emanates off her. It takes a certain lung capacity to breathe Ava in, and I thought I'd be able to do it. Maybe I was wrong.

Maybe it's me who's ruining things. Ava and I started fucking while she was still my patient, so it's arguable that I was the one who crossed the line. I knew my attraction to her was purely sexual, and I thought that would be enough. It turns out, however, it might not be enough for me. I know she has a spell over me because I'm addicted to fucking her, but the more time we spend together, the more I realize that sex is literally the only thing that connects us.

I thought that something else would've grown between us by now. I thought I'd have feelings outside the Black House. I thought I'd want more from her than to watch her come. I thought she'd show me she could bring more to it than that, and I thought I'd want to give more than just my cock and pleasurable pain. With all of this in mind, maybe it's me who's messing up the flow by having expectations that are too high.

All of it gives me a headache, which is why Excedrin isn't doing a damn thing today. My temples throb like there's a drum being pounded on both sides of my head, and as I sit at my desk and open up Tessa Milton's file, it only gets worse. Maybe it's the brightness from the computer screen or the thoughts of confusion swirling around in my head. Nonetheless, I need to get it together, because when it comes to my patients, I have to always be on top of my game. They don't get to know that I struggle with the same things they do. To them, I know my shit, full stop.

I take a minute to get my thoughts in order before Tessa shows up. She's a beautiful woman who's been through a lot with her ex-boyfriend, who I always thought was a real piece of shit. Now that things between them have ended, Tessa is trying to find her way out of the maze of societal opinions and judgments. It can be a tough task, especially when you've gone your whole life constantly doing what other people expect you to do.

My goal for Tessa is to help her break out of that, but it's hard to convince someone that the opinions of other people don't matter. In today's society, we're constantly flooded with the opinions of other people. Social media makes this ten times worse than it should be, and even if the comments and opinions are from random people that we don't even know, they still affect us. Breaking that cycle is a must for Tessa, just as it is for most of the people in the world.

After a few minutes of jotting down notes for my session with Tessa, I feel ready to get my day started. I stand up from my seat and stretch out, and even take a second to walk over to the couch my patients will sit on and straighten it out for them. I fluff the pillow and make sure the box of tissues on the table is filled up. Once everything is in order, I go back to my desk and wait for Keisha to tell me Tessa has arrived.

Instead of Keisha over the intercom, the next sound I hear is Keisha's voice through my door. She sounds agitated as she raises her voice, and then my heart drops to my feet as I hear another voice that I recognize. Ava's.

"You can't go back there, Ava," Keisha says. I can tell she's trying to remain calm, but she's pissed. "Ava, Dr. Colson has an appointment in ten minutes. This is not the time."

"He's my boyfriend, Keisha," Ava fires back. "I'm not a patient anymore, and I'm allowed to go see my boyfriend at his job. Stop being jealous and tell him I'm here. Or, I'll just go in myself. It's not like he keeps the door locked."

"Ava, you can't do this," Keisha retorts, but Ava doesn't care, and I'm stunned when the door to my office flies open. Standing there in dark purple leggings that hug her thighs and put her glorious ass on display, is Ava. She's sporting a black shirt underneath a purple and black jacket, with her hair flowing down behind her back. She looks furious at first, but when she sees me, her fire dies out, and she smiles.

"Hey, baby," she says, as if she didn't just burst into my office ten minutes before I have a patient.

Fuck.

CHAPTER SIXTEEN

Malcolm ~

~ M "Umm, Ava, what the fuck?" I whisper, almost to myself but loud enough for both women to hear me.

"Hi, babe," Ava replies with a smile, as she casually walks across the room and leans in to kiss me on the cheek. It's like everything moves in slow motion as Ava lifts herself to her tippy-toes and pecks my face. I look over at Keisha, and she looks like she's ready to fight both of us. She glares at Ava for barging in, and at me for letting her.

"Ava, what are you doing here?" I ask, pulling my face back so I can look into her eyes. "I have a patient who will be here in just a few minutes. You can't come barging in like this."

"Oh, I know, babe," Ava answers, calling me "babe" for the second time, even though this is the first day she's ever used that term of endearment for me. "I didn't mean to be disruptive. I just wanted to come see you, and tell you to have a great day at work. That's all. Is that too much to ask?"

Keisha, standing behind Ava, rolls her eyes so hard I think they might get stuck.

"No, that's not too much to ask, Ava, but I'm at work already," I try to explain. "And Keisha told you I have a patient coming, so this isn't good. You can't do shit like this."

"Well, I'm sorry. I just wanted to see you, that's all. Look, can we just talk alone?" Ava looks over her shoulder at Keisha, and the two of them exchange bitter glances. Keisha has never liked Ava, but now that we're together and Keisha knows how things began between us, she *really* doesn't like her.

I let out a tired, annoyed sigh, before looking up at Keisha. "Can you give us a second, please? Please let me know when Tessa arrives. I'm sorry, Keisha."

My secretary looks irate, but does as I request without saying a word. The second Keisha is out of the room, Ava turns to me and leans in for another kiss, this one on my mouth. Her tongue darts out and forces its way between my lips before I can even protest. While our tongues clash, Ava reaches down and grabs ahold of my cock, instantly making me hard.

"Jesus, Ava," I bark, as I yank her hand away and take a step back. "What the hell is the matter with you? You can't do this shit right now. I'm at my job, and I have a client who's almost certainly minutes away from being here. Why are you acting like this?"

"Because I fucking love you, Malcolm," Ava blurts, the words coming out in a hurry. "There, I said it, and this time I don't just mean how much I love your cock. I'm in love with you. I realized it when I woke up this morning. I thought about everything we've been through, and how I was ready to stab that girl at the movie theater just for looking at you."

"Which one?"

"Both of them! I was ready to be hauled off to jail for you, and I realized that's not normal. Only someone who's in love would be willing to do that. When I realized that's what it was all about, I had to come see you. I'm sorry that once I got here I got overwhelmed and couldn't keep my hands off you, but love will do that. I know you probably don't feel the same way, but I had to come see you, and I had to say it. I love you, Malcolm."

The world starts to spin like a merry-go-round. What the fuck am I supposed to say to that? I don't love Ava, and probably never will. I don't want to hurt her feelings, and I know how sensitive she is, so all of this feels like a lot of stress. The words I choose next have to be perfect because I don't want to set her off, but as I think about it with a dumb look covering my face like a mask, the words escape me. I stand there silently for too long, so I just go with what's in my head.

"Umm, I don't know what to say, Ava," I say in a hushed tone, hoping she'll mirror me and not blow up.

"I don't need you to say it back, Malcolm," Ava replies, with a shrug and soft smile. "The only thing I want to hear is that you want to be with me. It's that simple. Do you want to be with me?"

My head feels like it's spinning, because I'm torn into two separate pieces right now. I love fucking Ava. I love seeing the way the braids of my flogger kiss across her soft skin. I love the moan she releases into the air when I control her—when I pull her hair and make her look at me while pounding into her. I love the way her pussy feels when I cover it with my mouth. There's so much I love doing to her, but I do not love Ava, and at this point, I don't know where I am when it comes to being with her. Things are escalating, and the higher it all goes, the crazier she seems, and the less I want to do with her. There's something growing in me that wants more than just sex with the woman I'm dating. Call it maturity, I guess.

"Ava," I manage to say with a quick head shake.

"How about now?" Ava says, just before she reaches up and ties her hair into a ponytail.

"What?" I ask, truly confused.

"How about now?" Ava lets go of her hair, and slowly lowers her hands down to her pants. With eyes as wide as silver dollars, I watch as Ava slides her pants down to her ankles, before stepping out of them and tossing the purple leggings to the floor next to her.

"Ava, don't do that," I plead, as I keep stealing glances up at the door, even though Keisha has literally never walked into my office unannounced. The only person who has ever done that is Ava.

Without another word, Ava pulls off her jacket and lifts her shirt over her head, revealing her gorgeous breasts that were unsupported by a bra. She tosses the jacket and shirt on top of her leggings, and drops herself down to her knees. Ava's brown eyes lift up to meet mine, grabbing all of my attention as she assumes the position I love.

"How about now... sir?"

Fuck.

CHAPTER SEVENTEEN

~Malcolm ~

Everything in me wants her. Every fiber of my being, every follicle on my body, every cell that makes me human wants to walk around her naked body searching out places to touch. I want to spank her. I want to tie her to my desk somehow and fuck her until she screams loud enough to be heard on the sidewalk outside. I want it so much that I feel myself shaking as I try to hold back. I have barriers raised, but my desire is like a dinosaur throwing its weight at them, knocking them back, tilting them, keeping those barriers teetering on the edge of falling over. I have to stabilize them before it's too late.

"Fuck," I mumble, before clearing my throat and starting again. "Ava, this isn't how this works. You know that. You don't set the rules in this relationship. I do. Now, get up."

Ava keeps her forehead aimed at the floor and her chin tucked into her chest.

"No, sir," she says, nearly knocking me back.

"Excuse me?" I ask, frowning.

"No, sir," Ava repeats without the slightest hint of fear in her voice. "The rules have changed now, sir. I'm madly in love with you, and since you can't say it back to me right now, I want you to show it to me. I need to feel it deep within me that this is real, otherwise, I don't know what I might do. No one wants to say 'I love you' and not have it reciprocated. And I'm not saying you *have* to say it if you don't mean it, but I'm begging you to show me that you want me. Take me. Control me. Own me, Malcolm, and do it with your secretary sitting right outside. Show me you want me. Please."

In my head, I let out a scream. Ava is like an evil genius when it comes to manipulating me, and I know that's what she's doing. I'm fully aware that she uses sex against me to keep me close to her, and I know we wouldn't even be together if I didn't have an addiction that she feeds. The problem isn't that I don't know she's doing it. The problem is that I do know, but still can't stop her. Even when I know I shouldn't give in, my addiction wins every time, and I feel it ready to topple over my barriers right now. I only have an ounce of strength left, and I try to use it as a last ditch effort.

"Ava, you have to get up. My client will be here any second," I say, but it sounds shaky in my throat. It's weak and soft, because the confident, dominant side of me doesn't want her to stop. The dom inside of me loves this and wants to punish Ava for disobeying me. The *real* me wants to fuck.

"Are you my dominant?" Ava asks, and I gasp under my breath.

"What?"

"Are you my dominant, Malcolm? Do you want me as your submissive? Because the Malcolm I know and love would know what to do with this pussy right here and now. The Malcolm I know would punish me for breaking his rules by fucking me until I had to crawl out of here, right past your secretary and patient on my hands and knees. The Malcolm I know could handle me."

I don't answer. The barriers inside of me topple over and I feel my sensible side slip beneath the waves, just as I'm overcome with an ocean of kinky desire. I know what I shouldn't do, but I have to do it.

"Get up," I say, but when I speak this time, there's nothing but aggressiveness and certainty in my tone. Even with the voice she recognizes, Ava is still defiant, testing me.

"No, sir," she says, as she lifts her eyes to meet mine.

Before I say another word, I bend forward and wrap my hands around Ava's throat. She gasps as I apply pressure to the sides of her neck, making sure to stay away from her windpipe, because this is about dominance, not abuse.

"You know the rules, Ava," I say into her ear. "You know you're not allowed to come to my place of work and do this shit, yet here you are. To add insult to injury, you disobey me. Now, you must be punished. So, get the fuck up. Now."

I tighten my grip on the sides of Ava's neck just a bit, and use it to help her get to her feet. With my hand still in place, I lean forward and whisper into her ear.

"I'm going to let you go, and you're going to go over to my door and lock it. Afterwards, you will walk back to my desk and bend over, laying your upper body on the desk and poking your ass out for me. Do you understand?"

Ava gasps beneath my grip. "Yes, sir."

"Good. Now go."

I let go of Ava and watch as she makes her way over to my door wearing absolutely nothing. I watch her thick ass sway back and forth, and as I watch, I unfasten my pants and let them drop to the floor. By the time Ava turns around, I'm wearing nothing from the waist down, and my hard cock is out in the open, standing completely erect and jutting out from beneath my shirt. Ava sees it and licks her lips in anticipation. I know what she wants, but she won't be allowed. Not yet.

I stand at the side of my desk as Ava walks over and does as I told her. She bends over, laying her torso on the cold surface before arching her back and sticking her ass up.

"Higher," I demand, and Ava pokes it out further. "Good girl. Now don't move, and don't speak. You won't say another word until I grant you permission to."

Tempted to say, "Yes, sir," I hear Ava swallow the words back down.

I walk around Ava's body, taking in the sight of her. She's so gorgeous it hurts to not be inside of her right now. I want to feel her pussy pulsating around my cock as she comes all over me. However, Ava deserves punishment, so I'll have to forego my desires a bit. I'm limited because I don't have the entire Black House at my disposal, but I'm also constrained by time. Tessa is probably parking her car right now, so I have to get to it.

I approach Ava from behind and run my hand over her bare pussy. She gasps, and I allow myself a moment to revel in the sound before inserting my thumb into her. Ava releases a quiet chirp as I curve my thumb downward towards her stomach, finding her g-spot.

"You've been very disobedient today, Ava," I whisper, as I begin fucking Ava with my thumb while keeping it curved to hit her g-spot. "You have a problem with boundaries, and I don't like that. You claim you love me, but constantly break my rules. It's intriguing to me, but also annoying. It's frustrating as fuck. You're going to know what that feels like."

I thrust my thumb into Ava's pussy over and over again, and the sound of how wet she is starts to grow louder, threatening to escape through the locked door. I should care, but the dom in me is in full control now, and I keep going, fucking her harder and faster, until I see Ava's hands tighten around the edges of the desk. I know she's close, and I know when she comes it'll be like a volcanic eruption since I'm all over her g-spot. She's ready to let it out, and just as she reaches the peak, I pull my thumb out completely and take a step back.

Ava lets out a groan, and I know she wants to complain.

"Don't say a word," I snip before she can speak. "You disobey, and you're punished. Those are the rules. Now, don't fucking move."

Ava tightens her jaw, but doesn't speak. I can see how wet her pussy is from here, and I quickly step up behind her and slide my thick cock inside. Ava moans into the desk, struggling to keep it all sucked down, and it only becomes more difficult as I start to fuck her with a fury.

The beauty of Ava is that I don't have to hold back with her. If I were dating someone else or someone new, I wouldn't be able to shake the feeling that the person I'm with couldn't handle all of me. Whether it be the spanking, choking, flogging, or my cock thrusting deep and hard like a blood-filled piston, I'd feel worried about hurting someone new or giving them more than they could handle. With Ava, I'm unchained. I'm free to give her all of me in every way, and I bask in it each and every time I fuck this woman.

I fuck Ava with the strength of two men at once. It doesn't matter to me that we've been fucking for four months and dating for two. I fuck like it's the first time, every single time. I fuck like this is our first date and I want her to remember me forever. I fuck like I'm trying to impress her, even though she's already fully aware of what I'm capable of. I fuck like I don't want to be the best just once, but every time we're together. Each time has to be equal to or top the last time. There can be no regression. No excuses. No letdowns. I fuck in a way that makes her want to tell her friends about it, but is afraid to out of fear that they'll want a taste of me, too. Sex is everything to me, and if other men aren't doing it this way—if they aren't trying to impress their women every single time they fuck, then they're out of their minds and need to come sit on my couch for a few sessions on how to satisfy their significant other. I refuse to give less than my absolute all—no matter what time it is, no matter how tired I am, no matter how stressful my day was. She will get the best of me.

My cock thrusts in and out of Ava over and over again, and I can feel the desk starting to move. It scoots forward just a bit with each powerful thrust of my cock, and I know the sound is reaching Keisha. I know she's pissed about it, too, but I don't care. I'm too far gone now, and I can feel the pressure of an orgasm creeping up on me. My body reaches the summit, and just before I barrel over the edge, I pull out.

"I'm going to come," I say in a loud whisper. "Get on your knees."

Ava gasps with excitement as she gets up from the desk and drops to the floor. Her hands find my cock and start to stroke it as she sucks me into her mouth just before I come. Like me, Ava doesn't give a single fuck, and keeps her lips wrapped tightly around my shaft as I come. I quiver above her as she keeps stroking me, swallowing all of me without the slightest hesitation. My god, what a fucking woman.

Once I've recovered, I look down at Ava, who stays propped up on her knees with her eyes locked onto me.

"You may speak," I tell her as I reach for my pants.

"Now that's the Malcolm I know and love," Ava says with a giggle and wide grin.

I smile, even though I feel something else deep down. Whatever it is, it feels a lot like regret—probably the way an addict feels when they know they've just fallen off the wagon. I know I shouldn't have done it, but I couldn't help myself, and now I feel like shit. I don't even know what to say, and before I can gather my thoughts, I hear Keisha's voice over the intercom.

"Umm, excuse me, Dr. Colson," Keisha says, and I can hear the gravel covering every letter in her words. "Your patient, Tessa, is here. She's *waiting*."

I clear my throat, which probably only makes things worse because it makes me sound guilty. "Okay. Thank you, Keisha. I'll be right out."

Ava smiles again as she grabs her clothes off the floor and rushes to get them on. I follow her lead and jump into my pants before going over to my mirror and making sure I don't look crazy. Ava does the same and in just a few seconds, we're standing at my door.

"I'll call you later," I tell Ava, just as I place my hand on the door handle.

Ava smiles like a child who just got away with breaking the house rules.

"Mm-hmm," she says with raised eyebrows. "It's so good to know I can always coax that out of you."

I look at Ava with a stunned expression, and she reaches up and turns the door handle for me before walking out of the office. She saunters past Keisha with a grin on her face, and Keisha stares daggers at me once Ava is out the door. I don't even bother looking at her, because I already know what she's thinking. Instead, I look over at Tessa, who's smiling with her lips pressed together.

"Good morning, Tessa," I say, after clearing my throat again and hoping Tessa couldn't hear my desk sliding across the floor. I'm also hoping I can shake the frustration I feel from being manipulated. Again.

CHAPTER EIGHTEEN

~**M**alcolm ~

Tessa struts into the room wearing black jeans with a white and black crop top hoodie that shows her stomach a bit when she raises her arms. Her hair is loose and showering down her back, and her makeup is flawless today. It's not a requirement for a woman to have her makeup on point, but Tessa seems to have focused on it today, and it's obvious. It's a change from how I've seen her in the past. She's dressed comfortably, but she made sure it still looked good. I applaud the effort.

I, on the other hand, have to pull my shit together. As the two of us go to sit down, I notice a long brown hair on my shirt and have to rush to pull it off. My desk is closer to the wall than it should be, but it's too late to move, so I ignore it and hope Tessa does too. Plus, I can't help but think that the office is wafting with the smell of recent sex. It's a smell that is pungent, and one I usually enjoy because I'm kinky that way, but it's not something my patients should be forced to deal with.

Forcing myself to ignore it all and focus on Tessa, the two

of us sit down. Tessa places her hands in her lap and makes direct eye contact with me, and I feel like there's something different about her. She looks like she's gotten over the breakup with Brandon, and came out the other side stronger than before.

"So, how have things been going?" I ask to begin our session. Tessa flashes a humble smile and nods her head.

"It's been okay," Tessa replies. "But I think things are about to change. I think I want them to change."

"Interesting. How so?"

"Well, I have a date tonight."

"That's great."

"It is. I'm excited, but also a little worried."

"That's understandable. You just got out of a two-year relationship, and now you're about to start dating. I think nerves come with the territory."

Tessa shrugs. "Yeah, but this is a different kind of date, so I'm extra nervous."

"Different, how?" I ask, just before grabbing my yellow notepad and preparing to write.

"This isn't the kind of date where I'm looking to see if the person can be a lifelong partner. I'm not looking for a husband, or even a boyfriend." When I tilt my head in confusion, Tessa continues. "I went to Applebee's with my best friend recently, and while I was there, I realized that I've gone my entire life listening to what other people told me. I've ignored my desires every step of the way, especially when it came to my mother. If she told me not to date around because it made me look loose or like a whore, I believed her and made sure I stayed in a relationship. She's been trying to make me be like her for as long as I can remember, and I've gone along with it. But, that stops now.

"I've been my mother's little doll for so long, I don't even know what I like. I couldn't tell you what type of man I'm interested in. I have no idea what I like sexually, or even what constitutes great sex for me. I'm not sure I've ever had great sex. I barely know anything about myself, and that's ridiculous. So, when I set up this date tonight, I decided that I wasn't looking to appease my mother by telling her this next guy is the best guy. I'm going to be completely open and honest with myself. If I don't like the guy, I'm not going to waste my time. Maybe I'll even have sex for the fun of it. Who knows? I just need to learn what I like, then I'll go from there once I feel ready to slow down. Right now is about learning, however long it takes."

I raise my eyebrows in surprise and smile. "Wow. Well, I'm impressed and I applaud you. Not many people who've lived under their parents' thumb can pull themselves from underneath that pressure. It takes a strong person to break free and realize that you can do whatever you want in your life. I like it, Tessa. Good for you."

"But, I do have a concern, though," Tessa says, furrowing her brow a bit, and releasing a sigh. "While it all sounds good, I'd be lying if I said I couldn't hear my mother's voice in the back of my head. When she finds out what I'm doing, she's going to tell me I'm acting like a whore, and that no man wants a loose woman. What's your opinion on this, Dr. Colson? If I want to have sex for fun in order to find out about my likes and dislikes, does that make me a whore?"

The furrow in my brow is so deep it nearly gives me a headache. "Absolutely not, Tessa. Even if you wanted to have sex for fun just for the sake of having sex for fun, that still doesn't make you a whore. You're a grown woman. It's not illegal for you to do whatever the hell you want with whoever you want."

"Yeah, but in the eyes of society, that makes me a slut."

Now it's my turn to exhale. "Tessa, please excuse me for being so frank. But, fuck society." Tessa smiles while I go on.

"Let me explain something that I think is important for you to hear. Society sucks, and very rarely gets it right, regardless of the topic. Society judges everyone for everything, especially women, while usually giving passes to men for doing the same things. The word slut is used to attack women for their right to say yes to casual sex. It's used to shame you for doing what you want, as if choosing to do what you want is wrong. When you don't want to sleep with a guy and choose to be friends instead, society uses the term 'friend zone' to condemn you for saying no to casual sex. To top it all off, society then calls you a bitch when you call men out for almost anything.

"So, let's review. If you say yes, you're a slut. If you say no, you're a prude who puts guys in the friend zone, and if you call out this double standard and stigma, then you're a bitch. For a woman, you're almost always wrong in the eyes of a society that values the opinions and actions of men over women. So, fuck it. Take control of your life, and do what you want. Fuck society. Don't burden yourself with the opinions of strangers who don't matter and don't know you at all. You should feel fulfilled in a relationship, and also when you have sex. But, how can you know if you're getting what you need in those areas if you don't take the time to discover what you like?

"My advice to you, Tessa, is to be selfish right now. You're a single woman with no children, and that's great. Take advantage of the opportunity to do what you want. You're not obligated to live by anybody else's standards except your own. And for the record, if you're not sure if you've had great sex or not, that means you haven't."

The smile on Tessa's face is so wide it nearly reaches the top of her head. I understand her situation, and I know it's going to be difficult for her to let go of valuing her mother's opinion the way she does. It's very hard to break free of things you've been taught from birth. In a sense, it's brainwashing, and those chains are nearly impossible to break. However, if Tessa can pull it off, she'll find a world of satisfaction that she never even knew existed.

"Thank you, Dr. Colson," Tessa says, still smiling. I can see she's still thinking about it, but getting acceptance in situations like this is always important, especially when you're apprehensive about making a drastic change. Tessa will still have her mother to deal with, but I hope our sessions give her courage to find herself.

"You don't have to thank me," I respond. "You should thank yourself for finding the courage to break free of the box that society and your mother had kept you in. Now that you're out of that box, it's time for you to discover all that's out there. Are you ready?"

Tessa, still holding onto her beautiful smile, nods her head. "Yeah, I'm ready. Fuck society."

TEST FLIGHTS

CHAPTER NINETEEN

~ **T**essa ~

"Wow, you look incredible," the nice, young man says as I take a seat across from him. We're eating at Michele's in Dover Downs Hotel & Casino, and I couldn't be more nervous.

The man seated in front of me wearing a blue T-shirt and jeans, is Eric Saur. He's in the Air Force, and he asked me out after seeing me at Target. He's an attractive guy. Sort of skinny with thin, silver glasses and hair that's cut really short. Typical military look. He seems a little nerdy, but so am I, so when he asked for my number, I decided I'd at least give it a shot. Now that I'm here, I don't know what to expect, but I'm an open book right now and ready to take on new challenges and learn all about what I want. So, my eyes and mind will be wide open tonight.

"I can't believe you actually said yes," Eric says once I'm seated and comfortable.

"Oh? Why's that?" I ask, before ordering a glass of water from the waiter.

"You're just so beautiful, that's all," Eric answers, staring me in the eye as if he wants to make sure I notice his compliment. "I didn't think someone who looks like you would go for someone who looks like me."

I frown, because I'm not big on people who fish for compliments by putting themselves down.

"Umm, okay," I mutter, before speaking up. "You look fine, Eric. So, what's life like in the Air Force?"

At the mention of his career, Eric sits up straight and gains a few notches of confidence.

"Well, I'm an engineer for the Civil Engineer Squadron," Eric says, and I immediately think of Missy's husband, who's also an engineer, but not in the military. He's a civilian who works for the Air Force Base. "My job is to help design construction and maintenance projects for the base. I'm the guy who designs buildings and structures for other guys to build and maintain. I also deal with a little bit of budgeting, but that's the boring part."

"I see. That's interesting, actually. My best friend's husband works on the base, and he's an engineer, too. Do you know Daniel Backer?"

"I do, actually," Eric chirps, with a strange little chuckle. "Mr. Backer is a good guy. That's so cool. Small world."

"Yeah it is," I agree with a smile. "So, do you enjoy being in the military?"

"I do, very much. It was always my dream to serve my country, and it's the most important thing in the world to me. It's really all I care about. I'm a Captain, so that means I can become a General if I put my mind to it. It's going to take tons of work and time, and I'd probably have to switch career fields to do it, but that's my goal. I want to be a General. That'd be the bee's knees."

The frown I feel sweeping across my face is impossible to stop. Did he just say something would be the bee's knees?

"How about you? What do you do?" Eric asks, and I have

to shake off the annoyance still lingering from the bee's knees.

"I work at Milton Animal Clinic in Milford," I reply. "My father owns it, actually."

"Oh, that's cool. So, do you want to start your own career at some point, or are you okay with just being a dog groomer?"

I frown again. "Umm, I never said I was a dog groomer. I have a degree in accounting. I handle my father's business finances."

"Oh, okay. Whew. I thought you were just a groomer. I was like, 'Eww, gross.' But you actually have goals. Cool."

I stare at Eric coldly for a moment before pulling myself away and getting a sip of water.

On this quest of trying to find out what I like and what I don't, Eric has already given me a few dislikes. I don't like when guys make assumptions about me, my job, or my career aspirations. It's cool that Eric has a career in the military, but that doesn't mean I have to have a career in the military, or a career at all for that matter. However, I do like that Eric is driven, and I like that he's in great shape. The military's rigorous physical training locked that attribute down for him. He's skinny, but shredded, and who doesn't like shredded?

After a rough start to the evening, things between Eric and I pick up a bit. We have a decent conversation to go along with pretty good food from Michele's, and now that we're not talking about work or my "career", Eric isn't such a bad guy. That works out well for me, because unknown to Eric, I intend to use him tonight. Getting to know him, and learning about his job is all well and good, but the real reason I took this date was to learn.

Since my last session with Dr. Colson, I've been doing a little learning about myself. I'm talking about masturbation. To be honest, I hadn't really done it much before. I guess I always had a guy around to help out with that. Although, I did have to do it a few times to finish myself off after Brandon wasn't able to.

Now, I've been doing it for two reasons: because I want to, and because I've been curious about the type of visual stimulation I enjoy. It didn't take me long to learn that I enjoy porn where a man is strong and dominant, maybe even choking the woman a little bit. I like to see big cocks, especially when their owners are giving them a serious stroking. My god, what is it about a man stroking his cock that is so deliciously good to watch? I've had a few orgasms to that alone, but I've even also dabbled in gay porn. Two men fucking each other's brains out seems to send me right over the edge as well. Apparently, I like a whole plethora of things, and if Eric isn't up to what I have planned for him tonight, I'll have no problem going home and finding something muscular and steamy to watch.

After all the porn and therapy, I'm ready to move into the next phase of my post-give-a-shit life. I'm ready for the part where I become the "whore" my mother will certainly think me to be. All I know is that I'm not settling anymore, no matter how many names I'm called. I'm finding new standards to hold men to, and if they don't meet them, they'll be brushed off my shoulder like flakes of dust. I already know Eric isn't the type of man I'd want to be with—although my mother would push for me to marry a man with a solid career—but maybe Eric can teach me something else. There's only one way to find out.

"So, that's when I realized that I hate my father," Eric says, finishing up a story I didn't know I was ignoring until now.

I take a moment to knock back the rest of the red wine I ordered to go along with my meal, before looking up at Eric and hoping for the best.

"So, you got any plans after this?" I ask, and I can see the excitement grow in Eric's face. He lifts an eyebrow, curious about where this might be going.

"No, umm, I didn't have anything planned. You?"

"Not much," I answer, then I swallow my pride like the wine I just gulped. "So, you wanna go back to my place?"

CHAPTER TWENTY

Tessa ~

After having Eric follow me to my apartment, the two of us make it inside. He accompanies me through the front door blanketed by nerves that show themselves in the form of anxious glances around the living room. Before he manages to look at me, his face is shrouded in angst. I can understand that. I'm skittish, too.

Never in a million years did I expect to bring a random guy back to my place for a hookup. This goes against everything that has been instilled in me by my mother. According to her, no man will want me after tonight, because nobody wants a woman who is tainted with the sin of lustful pleasure. No man wants a whore. The audacity of a woman to think she can just experience pleasure whenever and however she wants. Who does she think she is, a man?

According to Judy Milton, today is the day I'll no longer be desirable to anyone other than guys looking for easy women to stick their dicks in. Well, if that's true, I guess I'll be single forever, but what I won't be is a woman who's naive and doesn't know what she wants. I won't be a woman who doesn't know how to or is afraid to experience pleasure because of outside judgement.

"You can have a seat," I tell Eric as I walk past the couch and head into the kitchen, where a bottle of red wine awaits. I grab it from the top of the fridge and pour two glasses while Eric sits down.

"This is a nice place," Eric says, getting through the obligatory compliments of my apartment. "You been living here long?"

"A little while," I answer as I bring the wine glasses into the living room and set them on the wooden coffee table in front of Eric. He grabs his and sips from it before placing it back down, while I pull a few gulps from my own. Unlike Eric, I'm not driving, and I want to let all the way loose. This is a monumental moment for me, and I need all the courage I can get.

I let the alcohol slide down my throat and settle in my stomach. After a couple of glasses at the restaurant, I'm already feeling nice, so this glass should put me in the perfect place to push my inhibitions to the side and say what I'm feeling. I take a deep breath and sit back on the couch, locking eyes with Eric, who struggles to maintain eye contact with me.

"Okay, so I have a confession to make," I begin, feeling every single nerve in my body. This is like trying to deprogram myself, and breaking the shackles of my mother is harder than people may think. I have a hard time breathing and have to focus. "I wanted you back here tonight for a reason."

Eric smiles at me sheepishly—a half smile without showing his teeth, because he doesn't want me to know how excited he's ready to be if my reason for bringing him here is sex.

"What's the reason?" Eric asks, furrowing his brow but still smiling.

"My boyfriend just dumped me," I admit. "I was with him for two years, and he just ended it so he could travel with his band."

Eric's smile fades and all that remains is the furrowed brow and a look of unease. "Wait, so you want to use me to make your ex jealous? Is he going to come here? I don't want any trouble."

"There won't be any trouble, Eric, I promise. My ex is long gone. He's not around to be made jealous, so that's not what this is. I wanted you here tonight because after getting out of that relationship, I'm anxious to find myself, and I'm anxious to do what I want to do. I know I'm risking being slut shamed for putting myself out there like this, but I don't care. I'm a grown woman, and I want to sleep with whoever I choose to sleep with, whenever I choose. This isn't a rebound thing, it's a what-I-wanna-do thing. I'm celebrating my right to choose my own life, and tonight I choose you."

Eric looks like he just saw a ghost. Not a normal ghost, though. A ghost that has scared him, but one he wants to fuck.

"I won't give you the wrong impression or make you think that we'll go on to get married after this. It's not like that. This is about sex for me, and if you can't have sex with me without needing a commitment, that's fine. You can leave right now. If you *are* okay with casual sex tonight, I'm right here. Just like it was my choice to sleep with you, it's your choice whether you're interested or not. No pressure, and no judgement."

Eric clears his throat and shakes his head as if he's worried this might be a dream and he needs to try to wake up before going forward. After he gathers himself, realizing he's actually awake, Eric's smile returns.

"Yeah, okay," he mumbles. "I'm definitely okay with that. Umm, wow. I... I don't know what to say. You want to just start right now?"

I exhale a loud sigh of relief. When I started my little speech, I wasn't sure what would happen once I was done. I didn't know if he would judge me, call me a whore, and stomp out the door. I half expected my mother to be right and for Eric's face to shift into hers as he scolded me about promiscuity. But I'm relieved to find that Eric is okay with this decision. If he is judging me, he isn't willing to let that judgement keep him from having sex tonight.

Instead of waiting for Eric to figure it out, I lean forward and kiss him. Our lips press together, and I use my liquid courage to be the aggressor. My tongue slips out and parts his mouth, and I can tell he's taken aback, unaccustomed to a woman taking what she wants instead of waiting for a man to lead the way. Nonetheless, I surge forward. If he decides to back off because he's not ready, I will press the brakes and let him leave me behind. However, since Eric opens his mouth and lets his tongue caress mine, I know we're on this road together.

"Oh my god," Eric mumbles as he pulls away to look at me before coming forward again. "This is incredible. You're so incredible."

Our mouths press tightly together while Eric finally finds his footing and becomes the one leading this dance. He pushes up against me and I allow my body to lean back onto the couch. My legs part and Eric takes the opportunity to slide his body between my knees. I feel his erection pressing up against my clit as we slowly start to grind together like we're on the dance floor in a club. Admittedly, it feels good, and I can feel myself getting wetter.

After a few short minutes, I realize that this isn't something

I'm forcing. This isn't something I'm being compelled to do. This is the opposite of that. It feels right. It feels good. This feels more natural to me than suppressing my urges. So what if Eric isn't the love of my life? My body yearns to be touched. I want to be craved, and I want to be devoured, and I don't feel like some cock hungry slut who's addicted to dick like heroin. I feel like a woman who's strong enough to own herself and go for what she wants. I feel powerful and ready for a night full of pleasure.

"Condom." I manage to ask between steady kisses. I say the word as a demand, because it certainly isn't a question.

"Oh, yeah. Hold on." Eric rushes to shove his hand into his back pocket, before revealing a thick leather wallet. From the outside, I can already see the outline of the condom, and I have to shove a laugh back into my belly before I erupt, because I haven't seen anything like this since I was in high school. Eric even smiles nervously as he pulls the condom out.

Once I see the condom and nod my approval, each of us takes a moment to undress. It's awkward, but both of us try to focus on what we're doing instead of what the other person's naked body looks like. I remove my pants at the same time Eric does, but my nerves don't allow me to glance down at his package to see what he'll be delivering. Instead, I fight back a blush and lay down.

Eric sets himself between my legs, and all I can think about now is how I'm about to break all of my mother's rules. She's going to lose her mind if she finds out about this, but I could jump for joy because I don't care. For the first time in my life, I'm not concerned about what she thinks, so I lie back and prepare to enjoy myself the way a consenting adult should.

"You ready?" Eric asks, making me think he's about to deliver something large and hard, and I nod so he knows he has permission. The next thing I feel is the pressure of Eric sliding himself into me.

I gasp at the initial insertion, then relax. My muscles tighten and then loosen, because while the pressure of having something shoved into you is intense, the size of Eric's cock isn't. I feel uncomfortable even referring to it as a cock. Eric doesn't have a cock. He has a penis. I didn't realize there's a difference until this very moment.

I feel it, but barely, and I actually look up at Eric to see if he's in. I can tell from how his breathing picks up and his face contorts that *he* can definitely feel it. He's actually inside me. It's really happening.

"Oh wow," he says, before flashing a smile that nearly makes me cringe. "Oh my god."

Eric begins pumping. His movements are bumpy and awkward, and while I can feel it, it's nothing to brag about. I'm not even sure what I'm supposed to do in this situation.

Am I supposed to moan so he feels empowered? Do I scratch his back so he feels more like a man? I don't want to hurt his feelings, but this is far less than I'd hoped for. Do I fake an orgasm just to get this over with?

Fuck that. I refuse to be the woman who fakes orgasms to satisfy men. I will never do that again. If he can't get me there, I won't allow him to think he has. He'll just have to get over it and learn how to be better, but he'll have to learn that with someone else.

As the thoughts race around in my head, chasing each other, I can't grab onto one. I don't know what to do, so instead of just letting Eric be horrible, I try to grind myself against him, hoping to get some clitoral stimulation by pressing my body against his. I move around, and enjoy the instant tingles of my clit being rubbed against Eric's body. Before I know it, I find a little groove and it starts to actually feel okay. I'm not going to orgasm from this, but I can at least get some satisfaction, and maybe this experience won't be completely horrible and a big fat waste of my time.

"Oh, wait," Eric suddenly erupts. "Oh gosh!"

Eric spits out a long, dry moan as he leans his face directly in front of mine. I'm suddenly engulfed by his wine breath and pure disappointment as Eric comes much earlier than either of us could've wanted. So much for a night full of pleasure. Once it's over, Eric giggles, before pulling out and sitting his bare ass on my couch, panting.

"Oh wow," he says again, looking up at the ceiling. "That was unreal."

I can't think of a polite response, and I don't bother trying. I simply lift myself up, slide back into my pants, and sit down next to Eric, who's still sitting there naked, definitely soaking his ass sweat into my couch cushions. Maybe I'd be okay with that if he was able to satisfy me, but since he couldn't, I just feel offended.

"So, umm, I appreciate you coming over, but I've got to get up really early in the morning," I lie, but I don't care. What else am I supposed to say? "So, I'm gonna go get showered and get to bed, and you can let yourself out as soon as you get up and put your pants on. Cool."

I swallow down the frustration and lift myself off the couch, leaving Captain Eric breathing heavily behind me. Before I reach my door, I hear him call out.

"Oh, okay. Well, have a good night," he shouts. "Maybe I'll see you around?"

I respond by slamming my bedroom door behind me. A few minutes later, I hear the sound of my front door being opened and closed as Eric lets himself out of the apartment.

Once I know he's gone, I take a moment to sit down on my bed and think about what just happened. I was hoping for something thrilling. Something that would make it all seem worth it. I guess the first lesson I'm learning on this journey is that not every man is capable of satisfying a woman. That's not on me, though. It's on him. So, my shower will be one of irritation and annoyance, but I'll wash all of that off and look forward to the next step. Whenever and whoever that may be. For tonight, it'll be my vibrator to the rescue.

Ugh.

CHAPTER TWENTY-ONE

~ T essa ~

"Tessa, you really should smile more. And why'd you wear your hair up today? You should wear it down, especially if you're going to be at the register."

My mother stands behind the counter to our animal clinic, glaring at me while I click the keys on my laptop. When things slow down with crunching numbers for my father, I try to come out of the back to help my mother with whatever she's working on. When she's busy with grooming, I help at the register if I can, especially if Missy isn't available. Missy is here today, but I'm mostly caught up with paper-work, so I wanted to get out of the office and come help. You're welcome, Mom. Thanks for being appreciative.

"Tessa, did you hear me?" My mother continues to badger me, ignoring the fact that I'm trying not to pay attention to her. "You're so much prettier with your hair down."

"I hear you, Mom. Geez." I scoff as I reach up and pull my hair from its bun, letting it fall clumsily down to my shoulders before dropping down my back.

"Don't pout, Tessa," Judy goes on. "We have to make sure

you're presentable when you're in the front. Plus, you're a single woman. You want to be as attractive as possible, because you never know who might walk through the door. Your dream guy may be just outside."

"If her dream guy walked in here, he'd be scared off by you nagging her, Judy," Missy speaks up, which always puts a smile on my face. If my mother is on her usual condescending, degrading bullshit, I can always count on Missy to step in.

"Oh, please," my mother says behind a scoff. "It won't be me who scares him away, it'll be that dreadful outfit she's wearing."

"Mom, will you just back off, please," I plead. "Your outfit isn't exactly fucking Gucci."

Judy gasps. "Tessa! Language. That's very unladylike. No man wants a woman with a foul mouth."

"Every man wants a woman with a *foul* mouth," Missy injects again with a laugh. "Foul enough to stick their dick inside."

"That is disgusting," my mother barks. "I don't like that kind of talk here. It's rude."

"You know, Judy," Missy goes on, ignoring my mother's cries for decorum. While she talks, I look down at my blue jeans and white halter top, wondering what's so bad about my outfit. "You just need to loosen up. You're too uptight. You're really starting to sound like one of those ladies who's gone a long time without sex. Is that it? You and Jack not releasing enough tension?"

"Eww," I chirp with a sour look on my face. "I definitely don't want to think or talk about my parents releasing tension."

"Yes, that's none of your business, Melissa," my mother snips. "Jack and I are fine, but that's not your concern."

"Ah, I see. So, *your* sex life isn't our concern, but Tessa's is," Missy keeps going. She's beautifully relentless. To this, my mother has no response, she just goes back to staring down at the cash register, even though we haven't had a single customer today.

As things quiet down in the clinic, my mind races back to last night. Even after a shower, I couldn't quite get over how lame my first ever hookup was. Missy laughed at me when I pulled her aside this morning and whispered the details in her ear, telling me that's how most guys are. Most men act like they're the greatest thing in the world, but rarely are able to live up to their own hype. While Eric didn't hype himself up to be anything special, I suppose I did.

I guess I assumed being open to random sex would surely bring great pleasure into my life. I figured I'd be sex crazed, stuck on getting my next fix of great dick like some sort of orgasm addict. In the end, the only orgasm I ended up having was the one I gave myself while watching a clip of some guy named James Deen fucking the life out of some blonde porn star. While the video was good and my orgasm was great, nothing quite beats the orgasm you achieve when being properly fucked. Unfortunately, I don't have anywhere near the level of experience in that area that I should.

The door to the clinic swings open at exactly eleven fifteen in the morning. Missy is standing at the register next to my mother, who's scanning today's appointments with a pen in her hand. After having completely caught up with my own paperwork for the day, I stand at the edge of the counter waiting to be directed by my mother, but everyone's eyes immediately jump over to the entrance when the man walks in.

He's tall, probably six-three, maybe six-four. His shoulders are broad, his face is bearded, and his dark brown hair is perfectly combed back. He's sporting a gray sweater that I can see his shoulders bulging through. They're like two bowling balls resting beside his neck, and his thick arms are stretching the fabric of the sweater. He's god-like.

"Hello," the man says, as he approaches Missy at the register. Missy's eyes bulge like she's staring at an apparition as it walks through a wall. "I was wondering if I could get her groomed. As you can see, she's a mess, so I didn't have time to make an appointment."

His voice booms like thunder cracking inside the room, capturing my attention, and I can't help but wonder how dick size and a deep voice correlate. Is that a thing?

I also have to fight back a laugh as I realize I was so busy staring at the man and his bulging muscles, I didn't even comprehend that he's holding a gold Pomeranian with the cutest little button nose, but it's hard to see because the dog is almost entirely covered in dried mud. She's basically a block of dirt with teeny little cute feet wiggling beneath her body. She looks adorable and gross.

"Aww," Missy coos, drawing it out. Missy is the perfect person to have behind the counter. She's always so fascinated with the animals people bring in. "And what's this little princess's name?"

"Her name is Coco," the man says.

"How adorable," my mother chimes, just before turning to me and raising her eyebrows, her signal that I should be interested. I roll my eyes, but inside I'm agreeing with her. Fuck yes I'm interested. Look at him!

"Well, luckily for Coco, we're not too busy right now, and we can certainly fit her in," Missy tells the owner of the filthy ball of cuteness. "Mrs. Milton, if you wouldn't mind."

"I certainly wouldn't," my mother says. She steps forward and takes little Coco from her owner. "Are we going with just a shampoo, or are we doing a cut as well?"

"Let's just start with a bath, and if anything needs to be

cut because of the mud, that's fine." The owner smiles a million dollar smile and shrugs his giant shoulders.

"Perfect. Give me fifteen or twenty minutes and I should have Coco fixed right up," my mother says in her best customer service voice, before taking Coco to the back.

The dog's owner takes a seat in the waiting area, while Missy looks over at me and bulges her eyes. Silently, we communicate an entire conversation.

Missy says, "Do you see how fine he is?" with her bulging eyes.

I reply with," Oh my god. Yes!" with matching large eyes and a head nod.

"You should talk to him," Missy signals with a tilt of her head towards the man.

I furrow my brow and shake my head, meaning, "Uhh, no."

"Do it! You're single!" Missy shouts with large eyes again and a sharp head shake towards me, as if she's throwing a dagger at me using only her forehead.

"Oh calm down!" I silently scream with a frown, my lips pressed into a thin line.

"What have you got to lose?" Missy asks now with a softer face, a shrug, and slight head shake. She adds, "He isn't married," by tapping her wedding band and shaking her head.

I verify the man isn't wearing a ring before letting out a sigh. At just the thought of talking to him, my nerves stand up beneath my skin. The man truly is gorgeous, and Missy is right, I am single. However, it's hard to get over my last sexual experience. Eric and his barely-there dick has me feeling guarded now. I know, though, that if I don't put myself out there, Eric will be the last guy I slept with for much longer than he should be.

"So, how long have you had Coco?" I ask as I peel myself from my place at the edge of the counter and step towards the register. I reach the corner of the counter closest to the man and lean against it.

"Only about a month," he says. "She's been a handful. Barks up a storm."

"Oh, yeah, Pomeranians definitely can do that," I reply, with a smile.

"Keeping your girlfriend awake with all the barking?" Missy asks, skipping the formalities.

The man laughs. "Uhh, no. I live alone, and have no girlfriend."

"Oh, you don't say," Missy says, and I don't even bother looking back at her because I can already picture her eyebrows raised and the look on her face.

"Well, she's really cute. Little dog in a big man's arms. It's adorable," I say, trying my best to flirt without making it obvious.

"Thank you," the man says, giving me that gorgeous smile again.

"If you're trying to pick up ladies by carrying the cute dog around, I think that's a good tactic," I state.

"Oh? Did it get your attention?"

"Definitely."

The two of us suddenly get locked into a sexy staring contest that I never want to pull out of unless it's to let him go down on me, because I'm dying for someone who looks like him to be good at that. Brandon was terrible, and Eric would've come in his pants just from thinking about it.

The handsome customer smiles first, and my smile follows, and it suddenly feels like Missy isn't even in the room. In fact, it's like the entire building is empty and there's no one but myself and the man whose name I haven't even asked for yet.

"Okay, she's all set," I hear my mother call from behind the curtain, just before emerging holding the gorgeous golden puppy. Now that she's free of the caked on mud, Coco is even cuter.

"Oh, you're good at your job. She looks great." The dog's owner gets up and meets my mother at the register, where he pays for the shampoo and the trim my mother gave Coco. He pays with his credit card, and as he's signing his receipt, he glances up at me and smiles again. I smile back, and am pleasantly surprised when he speaks up.

"So, I know this is a little forward," he says, spiking my excitement. "But, what are the chances I can get your number? I was kind of wondering if maybe we could have dinner sometime."

"You absolutely can have my number, and I would love dinner," I reply, my voice raising an octave. I write my number down on the back of one of our business cards and hand it to him.

"Thanks. I'll give you a call soon," he says.

"Before you call, you should probably tell me your name."

We both laugh together. "Oh, right. It's Scott. Scott Banner," he says, giving us one last jaw-dropping smile before picking up Coco and heading towards the door. "I've got to go, but we'll talk soon."

"Looking forward to it," I answer as he walks out.

"Well, look at you," Missy says as she comes over to give me a hug like I just won the lottery.

"Yes, look at you," my mother adds, but her voice is less excited. "Looking to replace Brandon so soon?"

"What? No, of course not," I answer truthfully. I'm not interested in replacing Brandon with another committed relationship. This isn't about that at all.

"No?"

"No. I pretty much just want to sleep with him," I say, making sure to add a giggle on the end to throw my mother off the scent of my truth.

"Oh, Tessa," Judy replies, basically clutching her invisible pearls. "I encourage you dating again, but I certainly don't encourage being promiscuous. That's very unladylike."

Missy and I laugh together, because if only my mother knew just how unladylike I've already been, and how I have no plans to stop.

Tessa ~

Scott gave himself a check mark in the "good" column when he called me the day after we met at the animal clinic. I was actually sitting at my desk in the back when my cell rang, and the second I spoke his name, Missy came running from the front to listen in. She smiled like a proud mother as she listened to me giggle and accept Scott's invitation to have dinner at his place. I thought it was a little fast to want to have dinner at his house on the first date, but Missy thought it was sweet that Scott wanted to cook for me right from the jump. When I got to his apartment in Smyrna, I realized why he wanted to cook.

"Steak and Stilton bruschetta," Scott announces once the meal is done and he presents it to me like a gameshow host. While he was cooking, I wasn't allowed to see what he was doing. He wanted to surprise me, and when I finally see the meal, I really am surprised.

"Oh wow, that looks great," I tell him as I lean forward and look at each layer of the little steak sandwiches he prepared. Scott has stacked sliced sirloin steak on top of ciabatta bread, and combined it with watercress, Dijon mustard, Stilton, and a few seasonings. It looks fantastic.

"Thank you, ma'am," Scott replies, smiling proudly.

"You're welcome. I'm impressed. It's not every day you meet somebody who can throw together something like this. I assume you're a cook?"

"You assume correctly. I'm a sous-chef here in Smyrna. Been doing it for years. I hope you like it."

"I'm sure I will. Let's get to it."

Scott brings our plates over to the table in his living room and sets them down next to the glasses of red wine that he'd placed there earlier.

Scott's place is nice, albeit a little small for a sous-chef making sous-chef money. Seeing as how he lives alone, I suppose it's fitting. The living room and dining room are so close together it's hard to see where each begins and ends, and the kitchen is right behind the dining area. All the appliances are top of the line, however, and the kitchen floor is black and gray tile with a dark gray grout. I can't see the bedrooms from here, but I'd imagine they're small and fancy as well. The dining room table is round and made of thick, dark wood. It seems to be made for two, and when we sit we're close together.

The first few minutes are quiet. The fact that we're perfect strangers makes things a little awkward, but as the food is eaten and the wine is consumed, we learn to navigate through how foreign we are to each other.

"So, how long have you worked at Milton Animal Clinic?" Scott asks to kick off the evening's conversation.

"Since I was a teenager," I answer. "It was my first job and I'm still there. My parents own it, and I'm their accountant."

"Oh, okay. I get that. What's it like working with your parents?" Scott asks as he chomps down on a piece of steak.

"It's like being confined to hell every waking minute I'm

there," I reply in all seriousness. Scott laughs, but I sip my wine, because it's only funny to people who don't have to experience it.

"I bet it is," Scott says, still chuckling to himself. "I couldn't imagine working with anyone in my family. It's hard enough working with people who aren't blood. Adding family into business tends to get ugly. But, if it's that bad, why not work somewhere else?"

"I don't know. I guess it's because I've always worked there, even before I finished my degree. Never really gave it a second thought. Maybe you're right, though. It's not like I don't have other options."

"That's right," Scott agrees. "You can be an accountant anywhere. Plenty of businesses need good bookkeepers and such, and I bet those places don't come with the added headache of working with your parents. I mean, we don't know each other or anything, but I guess it's just something to think about."

"And I definitely *will* think about it. For right now, I'll just keep thinking about how good this food is. My compliments to the chef."

"Sous-chef."

"You know what I mean. Anyway, so how long have you been a chef?"

"Sous-chef," Scott says, his voice suddenly sharper this time around. "Anyway, it's the only job I've ever had. I love it too much to do anything else. I'm thirty-three years old, and I imagine I'll be cooking my entire life. I wouldn't have it any other way."

"That's awesome."

"Yeah? Why?"

"Because you're passionate about what you do," I answer. "I'm not sure if I can say that about my job. It's just what I do. I'm not necessarily passionate about it, I just do it. You're one of the lucky ones who actually loves their work. I think there's a saying about not having to work a day in your life if you love what you do."

"Yeah, it's something like that," Scott says behind a chuckle. "I suppose I am lucky. I'm also lucky that my dog got so dirty, too."

I swallow a bit of wine as I furrow my brow. "Yeah, why's that?"

"Because I ended up meeting you," Scott answers, smiling. "I was excited when you walked over and started talking to me. The whole time I was sitting there, I kept thinking about how gorgeous and sexy you were. I'm too shy to initiate conversation out of thin air, though. I never know the right thing to say, so I was glad you spoke first."

I take another bite of the delicious steak while I try to gather my thoughts. The last time I had a date, I was more honest than I'd ever been. I told Eric exactly how I felt about why we were at my apartment, and I got out of it what I was hoping to. Well, not *exactly*, but you get my drift.

Here I am now with another guy in front of me, and I'm not sure how to go about telling him I'm not looking to be his future wife. All I want is companionship for the night, or if he's good, a few hookups every now and then. When a woman expresses feelings like that, there's so much judgement that comes with it, I'm hesitant to even go there.

I've lived my life inside of a box, and with Eric, I was able to break free from it. Each situation is different, however, so they each take special consideration. At the end of the day, the ultimate goal is to make sure I don't end up back inside that box. I refuse to be caged again, so that means I need to keep going. Just like Dr. Colson said, I'll be judged either way, so I may as well get what I want.

"Okay, I have a confession to make, because I don't want to give you the wrong impression," I begin, already feeling the shame I'm used to feeling from all the years of being talked down to by my mother. "Umm, I really appreciate you cooking for me and being so sweet. I've had a great time so far, and I think we get along, but…"

"Great," Scott says, cutting me off. "You're not looking for a boyfriend, right? You're just looking for a friend, and I'm already being shoved into the friend zone."

Dr. Colson's words about how women are judged for every decision we make comes roaring back to me, and I have to take a beat to regain my footing.

"No. That's not it at all," I answer. "It's the opposite in fact. I just got out of a relationship, and I'm not looking for anything serious. I just don't want you to think that this is the start of some fairytale where we end up living happily ever after. That's just not what I'm looking for right now."

"I see. That's interesting. So, what are you looking for?"

"I'm learning about myself these days. You know? Self cleansing. Taking time out for me, and all that feel-good stuff people say. I'm on a journey of self-discovery of sorts, and on this journey, I intend to learn about what I like and what type of guy I'm looking for. I'm fairly inexperienced, so I'm taking my time to experience new things."

Scott frowns and tilts his head to the side while he weighs my words. "So, you're in a hookup phase? Like, you don't want to be committed to anyone because you just want to be single and bounce between random hookups?"

"Umm, I'm not sure I'd quite put it that way."

"No? How would you put it? Because that's what it sounds like to me. You want to hook up with a bunch of guys to see what you like, and you came here tonight to hook up with me, right?"

I start to formulate a response, but Scott cuts me off.

"Hey, I'm down with that if you are. It's not every day you meet a woman who's just cool with a casual hookup. Most women are always looking for a commitment. This is every guy's fantasy."

Feeling torn by how the air in the room has changed to something much less comfortable, I suck in a breath before speaking again. "Every guy's fantasy? How so?"

"I mean, I hope this doesn't sound rude, but all guys think about is sex and how we just want to be able to hookup with a woman without having to say 'I love you' and shit like that. We all want that slutty girl who just wants to get nasty and then go back to her place like nothing ever happened. You're like the perfect woman."

"Slutty girl," I state, putting my fork down.

"Yeah. Wait, is that the wrong word? Is whore-ish better?"

"What? Are you kidding right now?"

"What?" Scott suddenly snips, raising his hands as if he actually doesn't know how offensive he's being. "I'm not trying to be rude, but you just said you wanted to be a slut. You want to fuck random guys, including me. Is that not slutty?"

"No, it's not *slutty*. If I was a guy, would you call it slutty?"

"Umm... Well, I don't know. Why are you getting so upset? I thought we were on the same page here."

"Because I'm not a fucking *slut* just because I want to like sex," I bark as I stand up. I get up so fast my chair shoots backwards and falls to the floor. "I'm getting so tired of these double standards. If I was a guy who hooks up with tons of women, I'd be celebrated by other men. But since I'm a woman, I'm ridiculed, even though a man would get points for sleeping with me. You don't see how that's bullshit?"

"Okay, I think you're taking this way overboard. I just *agreed* to do what *you* wanted. That's all. If you're looking for random dick, I'm here for you, and I'm not trying to make fun of you or anything like that. Jesus, just calm down. Are you about to get your period or something? You're way too uptight, because I literally just agreed with you."

"Wow. I'm so glad you showed me who you really are before I could make a bad decision."

"Who I am? What are you talking about?"

"Yeah, you're a misogynistic asshole who thinks every woman who enjoys sex the same way men do is open to being slut shamed and called names. To you, women are whores and sluts for doing the same things men do all the time. If I enjoy sex, I'm a whore. If you enjoy sex, you're a player and a ladies man. You can't respect a woman's right to choose, even if she's choosing the same things as you. You're a piece of shit. Thank you for showing me."

Scott looks at me like I've suddenly shape-shifted into another person. He furrows his brow, and I can tell he really doesn't have a clue why I'm so upset. His brain is so hard-wired into thinking this way about women that he doesn't even know it's wrong. He has no idea how disrespectful he is, and the last thing I want is a man who's that ignorant.

Without another word, I turn on my heel, grab my purse, and head for the door. Scott can't seem to think fast enough on his feet to say anything else, but when I put my hand on the knob, I turn back to him.

"Oh, and no, I'm not on my fucking period, asshole. A woman is allowed to have emotions *without* being on her period," I snap, as I snatch the door open. "And you can call me a slut if you want, but what does it say about you that I'm so *slutty*, yet you still couldn't fuck me? Goodnight. Enjoy jerking off instead of sleeping with me."

Leaving Scott with a stunned expression on his face, I walk out, leaving the door wide open so he has to pick his ignorant ass up to come close it. Once I'm in my car, I start it up and drive away, fighting back tears the entire way home.

CHAPTER TWENTY-THREE

~ *T*essa~

"Wait. He said what?"

"Yeah. He really asked if I was on my period," I tell Missy, as the two of us sit side by side at the bar in Applebee's in Dover. The place is fairly quiet tonight, which is great, because the only person I really want to be around is Missy. After all the drama with men, hers is the only presence that isn't annoying at the moment.

"Damn. Why do men have to be so fucked up?" Missy asks, just before tossing her red hair behind her shoulder and lifting her glass of Crown and Coke to her lips.

"I was hoping you could tell me since you live with one," I answer behind a giggle. "I had my hopes set on learning something of value in all of this. Instead, all I've learned is how disappointing men can be."

I guess I could've warned you about that," Missy admits with a shrug. "If there's one thing men can always be counted on to do, it's being disappointing."

"I think it might have something to do with their egos. I'm starting to think that maybe their egos are far more fragile than we know. Putting us down seems to make them feel better about their own flaws and inadequacies."

"Plus their tiny dicks and premature ejaculation."

Both of us explode into laughter, which feels really good right now. It's been a horrible week. Work is work, and that always has the dark shadow of my mother lingering above it. Brandon is still off with his bullshit band, probably getting his dick sucked by white trash groupies who'll fuck anybody in a band, and now my own sex life is stalling out before it even has a chance to get off the ground. The level of stress I'm feeling can't really be stripped away by alcohol, but it's worth a shot. No pun intended.

"In all seriousness, Tessa," Missy says after we're able to compose ourselves. "Even though it's shitty so far, I think you're doing the right thing. You're taking your time to play the field and learn about what makes you happy. I don't think a lot of women do that. People have a tendency to settle, and that shit sucks in the long run. Either that, or they get locked down before they even know what they really want. When it comes to sex, I had no idea the kind of shit I'd be into by the time I reached this age. Hubby and I were lucky enough to both be open-minded and learn together."

"Yeah? You guys learned together?"

"Well, when I say we learned together, I mean I had to show him quite a bit."

"Oh, I see," I say with a giggle. "But see, that means that you knew what you liked already. I'm not even there yet."

"You're probably closer to it than you think," Missy disagrees. "Women usually want most of the same things. You want good sex that always has orgasms in it for you. You want a man who cares more about pleasing you than he does about getting himself off. That's pretty standard. The only difference between us is how we get to the orgasms. Some of us like it rough, some of us like it a little softer until it's time to come, but the end result is mostly the same. It's not compli-cated. When it comes to sex, we want orgasms. The more the better."

I pick up my drink—a whiskey sour this time—and sip it before nodding in agreement.

"I guess you're right. It's not like I'm an alien that requires some sort of special love and sex that doesn't exist here on earth. My clit isn't on Mars. I want someone to touch me gently when I'm in that mood, and to fuck me like I've pissed him off when I'm in *that* mood. But, I also want someone who's smart enough to understand that women can be on the same level as men sexually. If I want sex, I don't want to be judged for it. I don't want to be called slutty, or whore-ish, or any other dumb shit men come up with."

"It's something you should talk to your hot therapist about. He's a man—a really fucking gorgeous man—so maybe he can tell you why men are the way they are."

"I don't think that fits into Dr. Colson's job description."

"Of course it does. He'll answer any question you have for him. Personally, I think you should get very, *very* personal with Dr. Gorgeous. I'd bet my entire life savings that he knows exactly how to treat a woman."

I roll my eyes as I take another sip. "Missy, there isn't even the slightest chance Dr. Colson is single and waiting for me to swoop into his life with my sexually neurotic behavior and never-ending confusion about what I want. Plus, when I went for our last session, I'm pretty sure he'd just finished doing something freaky with the woman who came strutting out of his office before my appointment. The room definitely had a hint of sex in the air."

Missy gasps and brings her hand to her chest, clutching invisible pearls. "Oh my god. I wish I could get a whiff of that. What'd the woman look like, besides one lucky bitch?"

"She was cute, I suppose. Had sort of a cockiness to her,

but also this air of ownership over Dr. Colson. She sort of glared at me as she was walking out of his office. She looked like one of those kinds of girls who's a little crazier than the rest of us."

"I bet. Dr. Colson could drive me crazy all he wants."

"Okay, I'm definitely telling Danny about your crush on my therapist."

Missy and I share another laugh and finish off our drinks. I order another one, because I don't feel the effects of the first one yet, but Missy says she has to go home. She pays the bartender and stands up, grabbing her purse and setting herself up to leave.

"You'll figure it all out, sweetie, I know it," Missy tells me, before leaning over to speak directly into my ear. "And just so you know, there's a very handsome, dark-haired man sitting across the bar. He's been staring at you since you got here, and now that I'm leaving, I think it's a great time to go over there and give learning what you like another shot."

My eyes wander to the far side of the bar, scanning for a handsome man with dark hair, and after skipping a few not-so-handsome men, I spot him. He's got a black T-shirt on, a full beard that actually looks like he grooms it, and a sultry mysteriousness about him. Sure enough, he's staring right at me.

"Oh, yeah I see him," I whisper to Missy, who smiles from ear to ear.

"Yeah you do," she says with a giggle. "I'll be looking forward to hearing all about it at work tomorrow."

CHAPTER TWENTY-FOUR

~ T essa ~

A few minutes after Missy leaves the restaurant, I manage to drum up enough confidence and liquid courage to make my way over to the handsome man in the black T-shirt. The entire walk feels like it takes an hour, as opposed to just a few steps from my side of the bar to his. When I sit down, I smell a sexy cologne climbing off of his shirt. Its strong, masculine scent makes my heart flutter as our shoulders brush together upon me sitting down.

At first, neither of us says anything. I just sit next to him, rubbing the sweat off my half-empty tumbler. I glance down at his hand and don't see a wedding band, and I start to assume he has a girlfriend he's in love with but thought I was attractive enough to stare at from across the room. Now that I'm close to him, he doesn't seem interested. I'm about to finish off my drink and decide between calling an Uber or a taxi, but then he speaks.

"Bartender," he says, raising a finger and grabbing my attention. His voice is like silk over gravel, smooth but deep and strong. "Can she get another whiskey sour, please? I'll take one for me, too. It looks good."

I furrow my brow and glance over at him. From here, I can see just how good looking he actually is. His skin is flawless and his beard is thick and full. He has a decent physique beneath that T-shirt, too.

"What if I didn't want another drink?" I ask, half joking. My tongue feels different than usual. It's looser or something. I think I'm tipsy already, so another drink might put me over the top.

"Oh, you don't have to drink it," the man says. "If you don't want it, I'll take care of it for you. I feel like catching a very strong buzz after the day I've had."

The bartender comes over and places the two drinks down on the counter, one in front of me, one in front of the man in black. He watches me while I glance at the drink and back at him. When I finally reach up and take the frosty tumbler, he smiles.

"So, you're staying then?" he asks, taking his own drink and immediately pulling it to his lips.

"I suppose I am," I reply, dragging the drink closer to me. "I'm Tessa."

I extend my hand, and he takes it. "Will."

"Thanks for the drink, Will."

"My pleasure. It's the least I can do for staring at you and making you uncomfortable."

"Who said you made me uncomfortable? Maybe I liked the attention."

"Yeah? Well all right then. What do you say we have a toast?"

"Sure," I agree. I knock back the rest of the drink I already had, and pick up the freshly poured whiskey sour. "What are we toasting to?"

Will lifts his glass in the air and lets it hover in front of me. "Oh, I don't know. Let's toast to taking a break." I frown, so Will explains. "My girlfriend just told me she wants to take a break from us. That's why I'm here drinking my sorrows away."

Images of Brandon standing in my living room dumping me flash across my memory.

"Ah, I see. Well, I can relate to that. I was dumped recently, too," I say. I have to fight off the wave of sadness that threatens to wash over me. I refuse to be drowned by it.

"Well, here's to being cut loose," Will says, touching his glass to mine.

"So, what do you plan to do with your break from your girlfriend?" I ask, sipping my drink.

"I don't know," Will answers. He turns and faces forward, but keeps talking to me. "I wasn't expecting to have things slow down. She said for me not to call her, so it feels like it's completely over. I don't know. What did you do when your guy broke up with you?"

"Whatever I wanted, and I guess that's what I'm still doing," I answer honestly. "We'd been together for two years, and the ending felt like a giant cement block was being lifted off my chest. Once I realized I was free from the weight of it, I decided to just do whatever I wanted. Judgement be damned. It's liberating, actually."

"So, you've been partying it up since you got dumped?"

I let out a painful laugh. "Not exactly. The single life isn't all it's cracked up to be. I'm pretty sure all I've felt since I started putting myself out there is disappointment. Between how lame guys are and my shitty job, things haven't exactly improved."

"Yeah, we are pretty lame," Will says behind a chuckle. He sips his drink again before placing it back on the table. "Where do you work?"

"Milton Animal Clinic. My father owns it, and my mother works there, too."

"Ah, family business. Is that really as shitty as it's cracked up to be?"

"Probably worse," I reply. I suddenly feel a strong desire to laugh, but I don't know why. "Working there feels like someone has taken my worst nightmare and forced me to live it as punishment for my sins."

Will laughs. "Oh come on, it can't be that bad."

"Yes it is," I snip. "You don't even know, *Will*." I emphasize his name and it comes out slurred. Yep, I'm getting drunk.

Will raises his eyebrows and chuckles. I think he's a little drunk, too. His gorgeous face is flushed red, and his eyes have a weird tint over them. If I had to guess, he's definitely a little faded, but goddamn if he isn't beautiful.

"Okay, okay," Will says, raising his hands in surrender. "I believe you. Don't like working with family, huh?"

"Oh, it's not just that my mom is a judgemental, pinched faced bitch," I snip, feeling much more aggression than I should. "The whole place is annoying to even stand in. I hate it there, and of course I hate my mother. Maybe it's her fault that the entire place feels like a giant courtroom that's filled with the smell of dog shit. I don't know. All I know is that the place is definitely a giant courtroom filled with the smell of dog shit. And fuck Brandon."

I start to think I should slow down on the whiskey sour in front of me, but have you even ever had a whiskey sour? They're so delicious.

"Wow. And I thought I was having a bad day. Who's Brandon?" Will asks. He seems genuinely amused at this point, but the alcohol coursing through me won't let up, and I continue to ramble.

"The monster that dumped me and left to go be a failure

with his band, American Armpits. Can you believe that? That's their name. American Armpits. He left me because he said I wasn't driven enough, but at least I'm not dumb enough to tether my dreams to a group called American Armpits. There's no chance that shit works out. What a joke. God, I hate him. Fuck, I think I'm talking too much. Am I talking too much?"

When I turn to face Will, he's looking at me with a cute little smile pulling at his lips. He's so freaking cute. If he would just make me stop talking and ask for my number, I'd practically throw it at him at this point. With the luck I've had lately, he'll probably just end up being terrible in bed anyway. Probably a premature ejaculator. Fuck my life right now.

"I like it," Will answers. I can see him fighting back a bigger smile, but I find it so adorable I don't even get offended. "It's a nice distraction from my own shit. But is it really all that bad, though?"

"Excuse me?"

"Well, I just assume you'd quit a place that's as bad as you described it."

"I can't just quit. Why does everyone keep saying that? It's not that easy when you've worked there with your parents since before you were old enough to even have a job. I'm stuck in the ugliest, shittiest smelling place in the universe."

"Wow," Will says, laughing again before sipping his drink.

"What, you don't believe me? You think I'm exaggerating? Because I'll show you how terrible it is. Well, I'll probably have to hail an Uber because I'm pretty drunk, but once I get a ride, I'll show you how shitty of a place it is. Don't think I won't, Will with the magnificent beard and sexy cologne."

Will laughs again. "Wow, okay. Then show me."

"What?"

"Show me where you work. I'd love to see it, because I don't think it can really be as bad as you say."

I frown, pausing for a minute and hoping my brain will talk itself out of this, but all I feel is the alcohol flowing through me, and my inhibitions crashing to the floor.

"What about your girlfriend?" I ask.

"We're on a break, remember? Haven't you ever seen *Friends?*"

I smile like a kid on Christmas, because I fucking *love* that show.

"All right then," I say, pulling out my phone to book an Uber. "Let's go."

Ten minutes later, Will pays both of our tabs, and the two of us walk out of the restaurant together.

CHAPTER TWENTY-FIVE

~ T essa ~

"See?"

Will walks into the clinic behind me, both of us on wobbly legs, and he takes in the sight of my place of employment and annoyance. When I see the room, it's nothing more than a shapeless box where I'm judged, which is why I compared it to a courtroom. Judy Milton is the authoritative judge and my father and Missy are the onlookers in the Gallery, witnessing it all take place for their amusement, while I'm berated on the witness stand day after day.

While I wallow in the emotions I feel every time I step into this place, Will walks in and looks around. He doesn't look affected by being here at all, like he has no clue how terrible it is to work here for my mother. He shrugs before turning and smirking at me.

"What?" I ask, feeling annoyed.

"I don't see what's so bad about it, and I don't think I smell any dog shit," Will answers.

"Ugh, I should've known not to trust a stranger," I reply

as I lean over the counter and lay my face on it. The cold countertop feels good on my hot skin. "It's a terrible place… wait. What's your name again?"

The room is silent for a beat before he speaks again.

"Wow, really?" he replies, just as his name snaps back into my mind.

"Will!" I bellow, popping my head off the counter. "I was just kidding. Of course I knew that."

"Yeah, right. Anyway, *Tessa*—I didn't forget *your* name—if you see this place as being so horrible, maybe you should really consider working somewhere else. I know you don't want to hear that, but when I walked in here, it didn't feel like a shitty courtroom, or whatever you called it. So, maybe it's just the way to you."

"Oh, god. What, are you trying to be my therapist now? I already have one of those."

"No, I'm not trying to be your therapist. I don't even know you," Will replies, frowning. "I'm just saying you should leave a place if all you can associate it with is unhappiness. At the end of the day, you're going to do whatever you want. I just hope that whatever you choose makes you happy, because I get the feeling that maybe you're not."

Combining whiskey sours with the words of a complete stranger has filled me with a rare combination of emotions. I'm sad, stressed out, and annoyed all at the same time. Will is right, Missy is right, and even Scott was right. Working here with my judgmental mother wreaks havoc on my state of mind. She destroys my confidence with her every word, which I'm starting to think is her main objective. I don't even know why I'm still listening to her at this point. I guess I'm just used to it, and I've been doing it my entire life. Some forms of brainwashing are nearly impossible to break away from.

I let out a cheerless sigh, which is followed by tears filling my eyes and sliding down my face. I know this is being spurred by the alcohol, but the tears that fall are real, none-theless.

"Oh, wow," Will stammers. "Hey, I wasn't trying to be mean or anything. I'm sorry. Please don't cry."

I take a deep breath, trying to gain control of my rampant emotions. I've been down this road too many times. I have to fight it, even if the liquor is giving my mother's influences newfound strength.

By the time I've pulled myself together, Will is next to me, wrapping his arm around my shoulder. I feel a strong urge to lean over and cry into his chest, but I resist. Instead, I look up and see Will's brown eyes looking down at me. Through all the bullshit, I'd forgotten how gorgeous he is. When I went to sit next to him, it certainly wasn't because I was looking for a shoulder to cry on. Now that he's close to me, I remember what I wanted when I first laid eyes on him.

"You okay?" Will asks, staring down at me.

"Umm, yeah," I say. "I'm fine. Thank you."

We look at each other, both of us stuck in a trance. Thoughts of what it'd be like to fuck Will flow through my mind like a dam has broken within me, and when I lift myself to my tippy toes to kiss him, I have no desire to restrain myself. For a moment, I think Will is going to push me away, but when I feel his tongue slide into my mouth and the strength of his hands pulling me closer, I know he wants it, too.

Our kisses are fueled by a strong combination of alcohol and lust. It doesn't matter that we're in the dark lobby of the clinic, or that Will is only on a break from his girlfriend. We move like we can't get our clothes off fast enough. Both of us know exactly what we're after, and we act accordingly.

My hands find Will's belt buckle and clamor to get it undone, while he leans forward and kisses my neck, letting his hands fondle my breasts. Both of us breathe hard like this is the end instead of the beginning, and when my hands finally find his cock, my eyes bulge.

Every experience I've had since Brandon dumped me has been a bad one, but Will is off to a great start, because his cock is as thick as a cucumber. I stroke it with my hands while Will moans into my neck.

In nearly an instant, I can feel how wet I am. I'm actually shocked by it. Will's murky relationship status, the fact that he's a complete stranger, and being in the clinic are all reasons that this is "wrong," but they're also the reasons I want it so bad. And I *do* want it. I want it so fucking bad.

"Condom?" I ask, still stroking his cock and praying he says yes.

Will doesn't answer with words. He simply reaches into his pocket and removes the red latex wrapped in see-through plastic. When I see it, my first thought is that it actually might not fit over his thickness, but my second thought is that he needs to slip it on right this second and fuck me until I forget how annoyed I am with life.

Instead of letting Will fumble with my pants, I reach down and unfasten them myself, while Will pulls his pants off and slips the condom over his shaft. Just watching him makes me even wetter, and once my pants are off, I don't want there to be another second before he's inside of me. It's like I need it, and my body takes over. I turn around, lift my blouse over my hips, and place my elbows on the counter. Will doesn't wait either, immediately slipping himself inside my dripping pussy.

My breath catches in my throat when I feel how thick his cock is. It's slightly painful for the first half a second, then it morphs into the most intense pleasure I've felt in a long time. Poor Eric was like a limp noodle compared to Will, and when he starts pounding into me, there's no question about whether or not he's in me. I feel every inch of it, and moans climb out of my throat, demanding to be heard.

Will fucks me the way every husband should fuck his wife —like she's a complete stranger and he's fueled by lust and a desire to be impressive. His strong hands grip my hips, and he pounds into me. I hear our skin smacking together and echoing off the walls of the empty and dark clinic. It's so intense, I put my head down and squeeze my eyes shut, enjoying every moment.

This is what I've been hoping for the entire time. From the moment I decided to go against my mother's wishes and do whatever I want, I've been waiting to be fucked like this. I wanted to be fucked, not made love to, and I wanted it to feel better than good. I wanted it to be intense and raw, painfully full of pleasure so satisfying that it lasts for days. From the way Will is fucking me, I know I'll be sore tomorrow and probably the next day, and I'm totally fine with that. I realize here and now that this is what I've been missing from my life. Lust.

Brandon was never capable of this. He was always trying to be gentle, which is fine some times, but I could tell he did it that way because he didn't have it in him to fuck me like this. He'd come too fast just from trying. Brandon couldn't love me while still lusting after me.

Not only did he not lust after me, I didn't lust after him either. I didn't fantasize about Brandon's cock inside me, making me wetter and wetter with his every stroke. I didn't crave having his cock in my mouth or to have his tongue slithering over my pussy. I realize now just how important that is.

Lust is hot. It's powerful enough to overtake a person to the point that they cheat if there isn't enough of it in their relationship. It's seductive and nearly impossible to resist, and since this is the first time I'm feeling it in its entirety, I realize just how potent it is. Now that I have a taste for it, I can feel my addiction for it growing with Will's every thrust. This is what I've been missing. Pure, unadulterated, uninhibited lust. If I ever find myself in a relationship again, this will be a requirement. I have to know he feels it for me, and I must feel it for him.

Neither of us says anything while it's happening. Will's cock continues to pound into me, and all I hear is the sound of our breathing. It feels incredible, and I suddenly feel a strong desire to come. I've been making myself come plenty, but I want something stronger than that. I need it to happen so I can know just how intense an orgasm is supposed to feel.

My craving for it sends my hand between my legs, where my fingers find my clit and begin to rub. All that masturbation has paid off, as I know exactly how to rub it on my own, so the added sensation of Will's dick thrusting into me is more than I can handle and certainly more than I'm used to. I rub hard circles over my clit while Will works from behind me, and I instantly feel hot prickles reverberating throughout my body as the orgasm draws nearer.

"Oh shit," Will exclaims. "Oh fuck, I'm gonna come. Fuck."

Will releases a guttural growl into the air, and the sound of him coming gives me the final push I need. I'm slammed by an intense orgasm that grips my entire body like a vice. I squeeze my eyes shut so hard I see stars behind them as Will and I fill the clinic with our blissful screams.

When it's over, the only sound left is our heavy breathing. We pant like we're in competition with each other, and I smile when Will pulls himself out of me to remove the condom.

That was amazing, and for the first time in far too long, I feel satisfied. All the stress of Brandon, Eric, and Scott has been washed away, and although my legs feel weak and wobbly, I'm stress free. I feel as light as a feather and ready to tell Missy what I know she's dying to hear.

Everything is perfect, until I hear keys clattering outside.

Will and I snap our heads towards the glass door, and everything good I felt is erased by the sight of my mother pushing through the door and flicking on the light switch. The darkness is overtaken by the light, and Scott and I are both literally caught with our pants down.

When she sees us, my mother freezes at the door, her eyes bulging. "What the *fuck* is going on in here?"

CHAPTER TWENTY-SIX

Tessa ~

I've never seen fury on my mother's face the way I see it now. She stands there silently, wearing black and white pajamas covered by a red robe hanging loosely over her frail body. Her hair is tied back, and her face is twisted into a scowl that sends a cold chill down my spine. She is absolutely livid.

Will and I immediately start to scramble for our clothes, both of us leaning forward to pull our pants up from around our ankles. Before Will can even fasten his pants, he starts to scurry towards the door, shuffling his feet. I can see the embarrassment smeared across his face like egg yolk he can't get off. While Will scrambles towards the door, my mother doesn't take her eyes off me.

As Will scoots his way past my mother, she doesn't glance at him once, and I finish buttoning my pants just in time to hear the door close behind Will. Through the glass I see him speed-walking back to his car, trying to button his pants as he scampers away. He's gone without a word, out of my life for good. Now, there's only Judy and me.

"Tessa Louise Milton, what the hell has gotten into you?" my mother begins, throwing in my middle name for good measure. Her feet are firmly planted in front of the door, and it looks like she'd try to tackle me if I attempted to leave.

I swallow hard, focusing on standing my ground, but I struggle to stay upright against the pull of my mother's influence. "Nothing," is the only answer I'm able to come up with, which sets my mother off.

"Nothing? Nothing?" she barks, taking two steps towards me before stopping and pointing her finger. "You are so unbelievably disrespectful, Tessa. How dare you bring a man into our place of business and have sex in the lobby! I stand here every single day. I put my hands on that countertop. You've defiled our place of business with... who the hell was that?"

I let out a breath so I can speak coherently. I've been going to therapy, talking to Dr. Colson to prepare for this moment. I can't back down now, but the room feels like it has extra gravity in it and I'm being weighed down. I feel heavier and slower.

"That was Will. I met him at the bar earlier tonight," I say, and just hearing it out loud makes it sound bad.

"You met him *tonight*, and you already slept with him, Tessa?" My mother asks, and I can hear the disgust wrapped around her every word. "What has gotten into you? Ever since Brandon left, you seem to have lost your way. First, you make jokes about sleeping with our customers the other day, and now you bring a stranger to your job to have sex in the lobby? Explain yourself, Tessa, because I'm appalled."

"I'm sorry," I mumble, putting my head down.

"Sorry? Sorry won't cut it, young lady! You owe me an explanation. You made a decision, now live with it. Take responsibility for your actions."

As she talks, I feel heat creeping up my throat from my belly. I've been taking this shit for so long, I've gotten used to just putting my head down and waiting for it to end. Today, however, has to be different.

"What if he would've raped you?" my mother goes on, fueled by my silence. "You wouldn't have been able to stop it, would you? You know what that means? It would've been *your* fault, Tessa. When you act that way, giving men the impression that you're easy, it makes them think they can do whatever they want with you, and it's your fault for giving them that impression. I taught you better than that. Now, lift your head up and tell me what the hell has gotten into you, because your father is going to be livid when I tell him. Answer me, Tessa!"

The heat from my stomach builds up until it feels like I have heartburn from holding it in so long. I can't take another second of this shit or my head will explode, and before I can even think on it any further, the words just come out.

"Fuck you."

My mother gasps.

"Excuse me?" she says, and I can tell from her tone that she expects me to backtrack. Both of us are used to me giving in. But I've officially had enough.

"I don't have to explain myself to you, or anybody else, Mom," I snip. "I'm a grown woman, and I can do what I want with who I want. This is my life, not yours."

My mother's eyes bulge to twice their size, and I watch her glance around the room like she's wondering if it's real or not.

"Tessa," she starts to say, but I cut her off.

"No, don't say another word. All you do is put me down. You sit there atop your goddamn high horse, judging every single move I make, constantly telling me how no one will want me. You go out of your way every single day to make sure my confidence is in the dumps. You live in this outdated fantasy land, where a woman isn't allowed to be a woman unless a man says it's okay."

"I do no such thing!"

"Bullshit!" I bark. "You just told me that if a man raped me, it would be my fault. Who the fuck would say that to their daughter?"

"I'm just trying to protect you, Tessa."

"Protect me by blaming me for my own hypothetical rape? What a load of shit. If a man rapes me, the only person who deserves blame is the fucking pig of a man who committed the crime. It doesn't matter how I made him feel, or what I'm wearing, or how many men I've slept with in the past. If I don't give consent, or even if I take it away after I've already given it, a man is not allowed to touch me. Consent is my choice, and mine only. That also means I can give consent to whoever I want, including a man I just met at the bar tonight. It's my body, and I can do whatever the hell I want with it. If you can't take that, I suggest you don't even ask me about what I have going on in the relationship department. Either that, or just don't talk to me at all, which would be fine by me after everything you've put me through. Maybe I'm wrong for getting drunk and having sex in the clinic, but the choice to have sex is mine to make, so fuck you, and fuck your judgment. I don't want to hear anymore shit about my goddamn hair, or the clothes I wear, or fucking Brandon. I refuse to live my life by your patriarchal rules."

My mother stands in front of the door with her mouth agape. The sight of it makes me want to smile, but I'm too mad to force a smirk onto my face. Finally being able to speak my truth to her is the most uplifting thing I've ever done. I could have another orgasm just from the satisfaction I feel right now.

"You're right," my mother mutters, her tone suddenly changing to something much more solemn. "I've forced my beliefs on you, and I shouldn't have. I just didn't know it affected you this way. We're different people, and I can't expect you to see things the way I do. But, at the end of the day, Tessa, you have to have some semblance of self respect. How are you okay with sleeping with random men you just met?"

"I'm okay with it because it's what I want to do," I reply. "It's *my* choice. If I was a man, you wouldn't even be asking me about this. You'd say 'boys will be boys,' or congratulate me on being a real ladies man. The word *promiscuous* is only thrown around when the subject is a woman. I'm tired of the double standard, and just because I don't want to settle down right now doesn't mean I don't want to have sex and experience pleasure. I want to experience it how and when I choose, with whom I choose, and I will not stand for anyone's judgment. Not even yours."

My mom sighs. I can see the pain on her face, knowing that her daughter is a grown woman. I guess that could be difficult for a parent. Regardless of how hard it might be for her to understand that I'm a grown up, she has no choice in the matter. She has to understand, and she has to respect it. Otherwise, there's nothing left for us to talk about, and I'm okay with that.

After a moment of silence that feels like it lasts forever, my mother giggles. "I only came up here because I thought I left my reading glasses. I didn't expect this." Both of us chuckle before she continues. "I'm going to do my best to let you live your life, Tessa. I don't want our relationship to fall apart over our differences, and I'm sorry if I made you feel bad about yourself. I would never do that intentionally, contrary to what you might believe. You're my only daughter, and I love you dearly."

"I love *you*, Mom," I reply, and to my complete and utter surprise, my mother walks over and pulls me into a hug. I honestly can't remember the last time we did this, so it feels brand new. If only I had told her how she made me feel a long time ago, I may have not even dated Brandon.

I don't expect her to change overnight. I know we're from two different generations, and we view things completely differently, but I realize now that it's my responsibility to make sure people respect me, including my parents. I can't wait around for the moment she realizes how terrible she's being.

People get stuck in their ways, and sometimes the only way to break them out of it is to be honest with them. We have to speak truth to power. Sometimes the conversation is difficult, but the hard conversations are usually the ones we need to have the most. I, for one, am glad I spoke up, and I'll never allow anyone to disrespect me ever again.

HAZARD LIGHTS

CHAPTER TWENTY-SEVEN

~ M alcolm ~

What a week it has been. As I prepare for another session with Tessa Milton, glancing at my notes, going over them meticulously, I have trouble focusing because my mind is elsewhere. I'm distracted, which I hate, especially right before I have a patient step into my office. My patients mean the world to me, and they deserve my best effort and focused attention. They don't have time to wait for me to get over whatever speed bumps my life is driving over. However, when Ava is the speed bump, slowing down is an absolute requirement that can't be ignored without catastrophic consequences.

I've only seen Ava once since we fucked in my office. We had dinner in a crowded restaurant in downtown Dover, and she kept asking me what was wrong. I didn't really have an answer, at least not one I could tell her. Ever since she left my office, I keep thinking about what she said as she walked out after fucking on my desk.

It's so good to know I can always coax that out of you.

Her words were like a splash of ice water over my sleeping face. I've always known Ava was manipulative, but I went along with it because I love fucking her and tying her up. I'm obsessed with watching her come, so I'd just roll with the punches.

This time, though, I was much more affected by it. Hearing her say it out loud, admitting to trying to influence and control me, hit me somewhere deep. All I can think of now is how she's trying to control me all the time. Every text. Every time we fuck. Every conversation is a ploy to manipulate me into doing what she wants. I see everything she does as a scheme to keep me where she wants me.

A typical guy would think I shouldn't be complaining about this. I have a woman who wants me to fuck her all the time. What's to hate? The only problem is I'm not typical. To me, this is much deeper than just having sex. This is emotional control and manipulation, the exact type of thing I advise my patients to recognize and never to allow.

The problem I'm struggling with at this exact moment is a symptom of avoiding Ava. She's been texting, and I've been ignoring her. I'll respond when I have time, but I haven't allowed myself to see her. I'm afraid my hunger for fucking her will take over if I'm in her presence, and now I'm like an addict in need of a fix.

I feel it in my bones. My body cries out for her, and my cock feels like it might explode if I don't have her soon, so when Keisha calls for me over the intercom, it's a struggle to lift myself out of my chair and walk to the door. I have to focus on Tessa. The ground doesn't feel solid beneath my feet when I walk to the door, but I make it there, and that's a good start. I've got this. One step at a time.

"Good evening, Tessa,," I say, when I open the door. My last patient of the evening steps into the room, shaking my hand with a newfound grip in her fingers. In fact, everything about Tessa seems new. She's walking straighter and smiling brighter. Her confidence seems sky high today, and it radiates off of her like she's holding the sun in her pocket. It seems one of us had a better week than the other.

"Good evening, Dr. Colson," she says as she sits down on the couch, crossing one leg over the other. She's sporting a sultry black dress today, which is interesting because it's a little on the nippy side this evening. Tessa doesn't seem to care. Her legs are like a mannequin, long and smooth, and given the state I'm in today, it takes real focus to keep my eyes on her face. Tessa has always been attractive, but today is next level. The non-therapist part of me wants to stand up and applaud her for an astounding glow up.

"You seem well," I say. It's less of a greeting, and more of a method of stalling so I can get my shit together.

"I *am* well," Tessa replies, smiling wide. "I've had an interesting week, to say the least."

"Okay. Go ahead and fill me in."

"Well, this has been the most carefree week of my life," Tessa begins. Her eyes seem to float towards the ceiling as she remembers everything she went through. "I went on a few dates, mostly bad ones, but that's okay."

"Is it?"

"It is," Tessa answers quickly. "It was interesting to see everything from a different perspective, and it was a good reminder that there are a lot of shitty guys out there. More importantly, I was able to narrow down a list of traits I'm attracted to, and I realized what was missing from my relationship with Brandon, not to mention every relationship I've been in my whole life."

"Wow. All that in one week, huh? Well, I'm interested in hearing what you figured out," I say, feeling more like myself the longer the session goes on. "So, what was missing?"

"Now that I realize what it is, it seems so simple," Tessa answers. "It's lust."

"That's an interesting answer. How'd you come to that conclusion?"

"Last night, I got drunk and had sex in the lobby of my father's clinic with a complete stranger who was on a break from his girlfriend."

My eyes instantly bulge for a split second, but I'm able to fix them before Tessa notices. It's not judgement, just surprise.

"It was good, too," Tessa goes on. "He was, umm... well endowed, and definitely knew what he was doing, but it was less about that and more about how hot it was. It was *lustful*, and when I realized it in the moment, I knew that what I was feeling was completely foreign to me. Brandon and I never had that, even in the beginning. It wasn't there on the other dates I'd had earlier in the week either. But this guy, Will, he was able to make me feel hot. I felt wanted, and I craved him. I liked that it was naughty, passionate, and wrong. It was like I was feeling something lustful for the first time, and now I know I need it in my relationships. Does that sound crazy?"

"Absolutely not. That's a great observation," I agree with a nod and smile. "I think you're right. Lust is a word that's used to describe something as if it's wrong or taboo. People often say, 'You're in lust, not love," as if lust is something that should be forgotten about, grown out of, or powered through, instead of enjoyed and used.

"When you feel lust for someone, that doesn't mean that what you're feeling is wrong, or that you'll never be able to add love into the equation. In fact, I would say the problem most relationships have is that as they start to feel love, they decide to leave lust behind, mistakenly disregarding it as some school-age notion that's immature. It's not immature, and it shouldn't be shed like a snake's skin to be replaced by something *more mature.*

"Lust is a great thing to feel. It fuels passion, and in my profession, I see a lot of passionless relationships who can't figure out why it's not hot in the bedroom anymore, and the answer is that they've left lust behind. They disregard it with sayings like, 'We're not teenagers anymore,' or mentions of how long they've been married. But lust can and should last a lifetime. Once you decide to settle down, you should learn to harness it and preserve it for your partner, not let it go. You mix it with your love. While it's harder to feel the older we get due to careers and families, it shouldn't be thrown out to make room for those things. It should be kept and used as often as our lives will allow. We should make time for lust, passion, and pleasure, no matter how old we get. I think you figured out something a lot of people go their entire lives never understanding. Good for you, Tessa."

Tessa smiles like she's proud of herself, and she should be. For someone who seemed so unsure of herself and what she wanted, she has come a long way in a short amount of time. If she can keep an open mind and stay on this path, Tessa will surely find happiness. It may not be immediate, but it definitely will come, and when it does, I believe it will last.

"Well, I appreciate the support, Dr. Colson," Tessa says. She switches her legs to make herself more comfortable, planting both feet on the ground like she's bracing for an oncoming impact. "To my surprise, my mother showed her first signs of being supportive, too."

I raise my eyebrows. "Your mother?"

"Yeah. After the sex in the clinic with Will, my mother walked in on us before we could even pull our pants up," Tessa tells me, but she's smiling as if she's unfazed by being caught by her judgemental mother. "You should've seen her face. She was beyond pissed off."

"I'm sure that was uncomfortable."

"It was, but I think it needed to happen. I ended up confronting her about everything, and she was surprisingly supportive of my opinion. She even hugged me, and I don't think that would've happened if she didn't walk in and force me to speak my truth."

"Wow," I exclaim. "No wonder you seem so different today. You don't have the weight of your mother's judgement on your back."

"Well, I'm sure it's still there," Tessa jokes, behind a giggle. "She's just going to keep that crap to herself from now on. At least I hope she is. It was great to hear her say she's going to let me live my life and stop being so pushy. I guess all I can do is hope she's true to her word. However, I did have a question for you after talking to her."

"Perfect. That's what I'm here for," I reply, adjusting myself in my seat as I perk up at the thought of a challenge.

Before Tessa can ask her question, my phone buzzes in my pocket. Without looking at it, I already know who it is, and I grit my teeth together to focus on ignoring it. Apparently, I forgot to put the phone in my desk like I usually do. I was too distracted to remember. Fuck.

"Before she was able to get over herself and let me live my life," Tessa says. "She kept talking to me about self respect. Like, because I slept with a guy I didn't know, I have no self respect. What's your opinion on that?"

"What's *your* opinion on it?" I counter. It's always good to know how the patient feels about something before I give my assessment, just to make sure they don't simply latch onto what I have to say.

"I'm not sure," Tessa admits, shrugging. "I mean, I know my worth, but I guess I've always heard that people who sleep with random people don't respect themselves. It's something society tells us all the time. I just don't know how the two relate to each other at all."

"Well, people say a lot about things they don't really understand," I reply, ignoring another buzz from my phone. "Self respect has nothing to do with sex or nudity. Self respect means making choices that make *you* happy. Being sexual has nothing to do with self respect. As long as you're happy with your decisions—sleeping with people of your choosing, at a time of your choosing—you have self respect. It's as simple as that. Any other definition of the phrase is subjective—the person using it defines it by their own judgements and standards. Self respect isn't something that can be defined by anyone other than yourself. That's why it's called *self* respect."

Another beautiful smile shows itself on Tessa's face, and I can tell she's had a real awakening. Today, she seems like a whole new woman, and I'm proud of her for coming so far, and not being afraid to stand her ground. Breaking cycles created by parents is a very difficult thing to do, and Tessa seems to have managed to snap herself out of the cuffs that were placed on her wrists by her mother. I'm impressed.

"I agree," Tessa says, smiling as her mouth speaks the words. "Well, now that it's all said and done, I think I'm ready for whatever life throws my way. Sex, commitment, whatever. I've given absolutely zero thought to replacing Brandon, but I'm feeling open. If Judy Milton is able to stay out of my business, I think I'll enjoy playing the field until I find someone special."

"None of the men you spent time with this week will hit the jackpot, huh?" I ask playfully.

"Nah," Tessa says. "Will was definitely good last night at the clinic, but I'm pretty sure my mother scared him off. Not to mention he was only on a break from his girlfriend. He's probably stressed enough trying to keep her from finding out what we did."

"So, you're just doing you," I state. "No need to dive any deeper than that. Just do you, and whatever happens, happens. Your focus from here on out should be on whatever makes *you* happy. Combine that with what you told me about the importance of lust in a relationship, and I think sooner or later you're going to find yourself very happy."

Tessa smiles her fullest smile of the evening as she looks at me. "I like the sound of that. Thank you, Dr. Colson."

CHAPTER TWENTY-EIGHT

~ **M**alcolm ~

Ava: *I miss you.*

Ava: *Do you miss me?*

Ava: *Malcolm*

Ava: *How is work going today?*

Ava: *I wish I could see you*

Ava: *You'd answer me if you knew what I was doing to my pussy right now. If I keep it up, I'll come all over my phone. You know I can make such a mess.*

Ava: *I'm much messier with you, though.*

Ava: *Malcolm.*

Looking at my phone after Tessa leaves, I'm shocked by what I see. My phone vibrated so much, I didn't even realize how many times it had been. Jesus Christ, what has gotten into this woman?

I finish cleaning up the area where my patients sit by spraying Lysol all over the couch and pillow. It's a disinfectant, to make sure no one ends up getting sick from having a session with me.

Once the couch is wiped down, I walk back over to my desk, setting my phone on the wood top and taking a seat in my chair. I click my computer and go to Tessa Milton's file, where I input notes from today's session. This won't be our last time seeing each other, but after the tremendous amount of progress Tessa made over the past few sessions, I think our time together is starting to wind down. She's on track to be happier than most people who sit on my couch, so unless she wants to continue therapy even after she's in a relationship, we'll be done soon.

After entering my notes for Tessa, I press the button on the intercom to reach out to Keisha, who hasn't left yet. I assume she's finishing up her own notes for the day.

"Hey, Keisha, you still out there?" I ask, just as my phone buzzes again. Of course it's Ava.

Ava: *Malcolm, I want to see you. When can I?*

"Yes, I'm here, Dr. Colson," Keisha replies. My eyes stay glued to the message from Ava. "Just finishing up. Do you have anything else for me tonight?"

"No, you're good. Have a good night," I reply. "And Keisha, thanks for everything you do. I appreciate you."

"It's my pleasure, Dr. Colson," Keisha answers. "Have a good night."

Once I know Keisha is gone, I pick my phone up off the table and call Ava. While it rings, I put the phone on speaker and set it down on the desk, leaning back in my chair, trying my best to relax.

"I missed you," Ava says the second she's on the phone. "Can I meet you at the Black House?"

Thoughts of the Black House race around my head like NASCAR drivers, and my cock instantly stiffens. It's been a while since I've had her down there, and I want it. If only Ava wasn't so... Ava. I lick my lips and force the images of the Black House to the back of my mind.

"No," I answer firmly. "I've had a long day, and I'm not in the mood for company tonight, Ava."

There's only silence on the other end of the phone.

"And you can't text me like that when I'm seeing a patient," I go on. "It makes me look very unprofessional. You know the rules."

"Yes, I know the rules," Ava finally says. "But I miss you, and you've been avoiding me, Malcolm. I can tell. I don't like being avoided."

"I've got a lot on my mind right now, so I'm taking the time to get myself together—to figure some things out. All right?"

Silence again.

"Stay patient, Ava," I tell her, although I know this is misleading. Telling Ava to stay patient implies we'll be back to normal soon, but the more I think about it, the less likely that's true.

"Okay," Ava responds, but her voice is different. It's deeper. More alarming.

"Thank you, I'll talk to you again soon. Have a good night."

Ava doesn't respond before she ends the call.

As Ava's former therapist, I know so much about her and her mentality, I can't help but feel nervous about the way she acts sometimes. She's a gorgeous woman, and I love her sexuality, but I know she needs continuous therapy from a psychologist, not a sex therapist. She needs to talk to someone who can help her with the things that run around in her head, and I can't do that. I'm not qualified to...

My thoughts are interrupted by another text notification on my phone. At first, I'm annoyed that Ava is still texting after I just told her to be patient. However, when I look at the phone, I see that it's not a text message. It's a photo—a photo of Ava's bare pussy.

I gasp at the sight of it, because I've been struggling to keep myself away from her, and this is the type of thing that's only going to make it worse. Before I can figure out how to respond, another photo appears. In this one, Ava has two fingers in her pussy, and I can tell she's wetter in this photo than the last one. She's masturbating and using it to entice me.

The next thing that comes through is a short video. It's only thirty seconds long, but it's of Ava rubbing her clit with two fingers. She moves in small, rigid circles, and I can tell what's about to happen from the way her body is tightened. Her legs are stiff and her eyes are closed. She's biting her lip, and I can hear her breathing starting to peak. Then, she comes hard and loud. Her body shakes so much the video blurs the last five seconds before she turns it off.

By the time the video is finished playing, I'm breathing hard like I just came. Ava knows the type of man I am, and she knows how to use it against me. She has also broken a rule by bringing herself to orgasm, something she knows she's not allowed to do. She can edge with my permission, but she's not supposed to come. She's pushing me on purpose, and from how hard my cock is throbbing, it's working.

I want to call her. I want to fuck her. I want to drag her into the Black House and tie her to the bed while I take my time using every toy at my disposal, until she comes fifty times and passes out from the bliss. I want it more than I can stand, and if I don't do something, I feel like I'm going to crack. So, I take advantage of the fact that Keisha is gone, and slide my hand down my pants.

My cock is as hard as any time I can remember, and although I don't usually masturbate, I'm going to enjoy it tonight. I open my phone and press play on Ava's video again, stroking my cock while she rubs her pussy. I can't come in thirty seconds, but when I play the video a second time, I end up coming at the same time Ava does in the video.

I get myself cleaned up, taking extra time to inspect the floor and desk to make sure I haven't left any evidence behind. The last thing I need is a patient's brow furrowing as they notice hardened cum on the floor during a session.

I also don't need Ava knowing that I masturbated to her video, so when I leave, I do it without replying to her. I shove my phone in my pocket, turn off the lights, and walk out.

CHAPTER TWENTY-NINE

~ **M**alcolm ~

Do you ever feel like someone is watching you? You know those moments when you're doing something mundane, something completely normal, then you get that nagging feeling in your gut. You get something that feels like a tug at the bottom of your shirt, something like a warning, like a Spidey Sense. Well, I just got it.

Standing in my living room, I hold three pieces of mail in my hand. Two of them are credit card companies trying to reach out and ruin my good credit. The other is a statement for my mortgage. I still owe six figures on my house. Thanks for the reminder, mortgage people. When I toss the mail onto the coffee table, that's when I hear it.

There's a tap at one of my windows in the living room. It's not continuous, so I can't follow the sound. It only happens once, just enough to draw my attention. My head snaps up and to the right. My blinds are closed, but there's a tiny sliver of darkness peeking inside from the bottom of the blinds where one of the slats is stuck on the cord. If there's darkness sneaking in, that means someone can see through that spot if they try hard enough. Someone like Ava.

Forgetting about the mail, I dart over to the window, drop to my knees and shove my face into the blinds. Only darkness greets me. There's no extra people walking around outside. No mysterious cars parked at the end of my driveway. Ava isn't here. I suppose it's just my imagination.

I lift myself off the floor and try to shake off the fact that I feel like an idiot. Why am I so paranoid? I've let my time as Ava's therapist take control of my mind and start playing tricks on me.

It's understandable. Ava stalked her most recent boyfriend, and was accused of trying to burn his house down. That kind of thing tends to stick with you, even after the therapy is over and the sex has begun. Nonetheless, I brush it off and try to settle myself in for the night.

I walk over to my fireplace and fire it up. The flames start low and build themselves up like orange bodybuilders right before my eyes, glowing bigger and brighter by the second. As the fire starts to crackle, I hear another tap from behind me. This one from a different window.

Was it a tap at the window, or the crackle of the wooden logs as they burn in the fireplace? Damn it. I'm stressing myself out. At least, that's what I tell myself when I get up from the fireplace and start walking to the kitchen, where I plan to pour myself a rather strong drink of vodka. However, before I can leave the living room, I hear another tap at the window.

"What the fuck?" I mumble to myself. I'm instantly filled with a combination of anxiety and annoyance, because no one likes feeling afraid. "Fuck this," I snap, then I walk to the window and yank on the cord, sending the blinds shooting towards the top of the window frame.

"What the fuck!" I scream, as a darkened silhouette of Ava stares back at me.

When she sees me, Ava jumps back, surprised by my opening the window so quickly. Once we both realize what just happened, we stare at each other, our bodies still separated by the window pane. Ava's mouth slowly curls into a playful smile, while my brow morphs into a deep furrow.

"What the fuck, Ava!" I yell through the glass. Ava's smile vanishes.

Like an angry teenager, I stomp through the house, making my way to the front door. I grab the knob and snatch it open, where I find Ava sauntering towards me with her arms outstretched like she's asking for a hug. She has on basketball shorts and a white tank top in this cold weather. What the hell?

"Ava, what the fuck are you doing here?" I yell. I'm so pissed off, it takes everything in me to keep my voice low enough not to alert my neighbors.

"I wanted to see you," Ava replies in a completely normal tone, dropping her arms to her sides and pouting. She acts like her presence here is totally normal and had been planned by both of us.

"So you decided to show up here unannounced and peek into my windows?" I growl.

"I just wanted to make sure you were home before I knocked on the door," Ava says, still sounding unaffected. "I didn't mean to startle you, and I can tell I did. Look how mad you are. I've never seen you this way before. It's deep. I kind of like it."

Without a single care in the world, Ava steps forward and tries to wrap her arms around my neck. I have to physically stop her to keep her from grabbing me.

"Ava, stop it!" I bark. "What the fuck is wrong with you right now? Do you not realize how you're acting?"

Ava pauses, coming to a complete stop as if she's been frozen in place.

"How am I acting, Malcolm?" she asks, her gaze turning cold.

I let out a sigh and quickly gather my thoughts. I can't say the wrong thing right now, so I shift gears and go into therapist mode.

"I don't mean to say you're acting in any particular way that can be labeled by a specific word," I say, trying to use my education in my career field to defuse the situation. Maybe I should've left my relationship with Ava as therapist and patient after all. I'm not sure we'll ever be past those roles. "You have to understand and respect boundaries, Ava. That's all I'm trying to get you to understand."

"No," Ava mumbles, taking a step back. "You were going to tell me I'm acting crazy, weren't you? Is that it, motherfucker? You think I'm crazy?"

"What?" I say, shocked by Ava's sudden display of anger. Before my eyes, the skin on Ava's neck starts to turn pink. She's literally heating up with rage. "I'm not saying that, Ava. I would never say that about you."

"Why? Because I'm crazy and you're afraid of me?" she barks.

Yes.

"Of course not," I lie. "I know you better than that. I wouldn't ever call you that."

"But you're thinking it."

"That's not fair. You can't make assumptions on what I'm thinking, and then use those assumptions to get more upset. It's irrational."

"Oh, so now I'm *irrational*?"

Fuck, I stepped right into that one.

"Come one, Ava. You're putting me in lose-lose situations,

and I don't like it. We can't work like this. This just won't work."

As the words flow, the thoughts flow with them. I knew this thing with Ava wouldn't last forever. It was made out of a situation that never should've happened. I was Ava's therapist, and I never should've crossed that line. It's my fault things are out of sync now. It's a rule you don't break, a line you don't cross, and I hopped right over it with no regard to how it might affect Ava. It's on me. And now I have to fix it.

Ava stares at me, glaring at me with an intimidating intensity in her round brown eyes. I know she won't react well to this, but I have to do it, because I can't keep this up. It must be done.

"Ava," I say after releasing a breath. I stand up straight and exhale again. "We can't keep doing this. We have to end it. I can't keep dragging this out with you, because it's not fair to either of us." Ava doesn't move or respond in any way. "I don't mean to hurt you, and I'd be lying if I said I hadn't thought about it before. I'm sorry, but we have to end this thing between us. It never should've started in the first place."

Suddenly, Ava smiles as if I never said anything. I'm taken aback by her quick change of mood, and I'm downright shocked when she steps forward again and tries to kiss me. I have to put my hand on her chest to hold her back once again.

"Ava, no," I say, firmly. "This isn't a game, and it's not some kind of test. I'm serious. This isn't about the Black House. This isn't about the rules. It's about me and how I feel, and this has to end. It has to be over."

"Malcolm," Ava says in a soft, pleading voice. Almost as if she doesn't believe me. "Come on. We're in love. There isn't anything we can't work through."

"No, Ava, we're not in love. We have fantastic sex, and I'm

grateful for that. It was phenomenal while it lasted, but I'm not sure it's ever been anything more than that, and that's just not good enough for me anymore. It's not worth it. So, this has to be it. Let's not drag it out any further than this moment. Please."

Ava stands in front of me, frozen again. Her eyes lock onto mine, and she barely blinks.

"I'm sorry, Ava, but it's over," I say again, just to make sure she really hears me. I'm not sure if she does, because she doesn't even move. She stands in front of me with a blank expression on her beautiful face as I take a step back and place my hand on the doorknob.

After thirty seconds, I try to snap her out of it. "Ava, are you okay?"

No response.

"Ava, please. I don't want this to be..."

"Fine," Ava finally says, spitting the word out like she hates its taste. After speaking, she's back to being frozen.

"Okay," I reply, waiting for her to leave, but she doesn't. "Well, I'm going to go. Take care of yourself, Ava."

Instead of adding more time to this awkward situation, I slowly close the door. As it latches, Ava doesn't move a single muscle. I shut the door completely and make sure to lock it before moving over to the window and looking out. Ava stays in front of the door, unmoving, for another sixty seconds. Her eyes stay glued to the outside of my front door, unblinking for an entire minute before finally stepping back. She moves like her feet are stuck in quicksand, but she slowly turns around and walks away.

I watch her walk out of my driveway and turn down the sidewalk. Down the street where I can barely see her from this angle, Ava climbs into her car. She'd parked nearly four houses down, which is why I hadn't seen her car in the driveway before. She was sneaking up on me on purpose.

Ava sits in the car another thirty seconds without moving,

her face being lit up by the light above her rearview mirror, and I'm absolutely stunned when she explodes into a rage, punching and slapping her steering wheel over and over again. Her mouth twists into a terrifying, inaudible scream as she beats the steering wheel with clenched fists, before slamming her forehead on the wheel two times. She hits her head so hard I'm surprised she doesn't knock herself out. My heart pounds in my chest just watching her.

"Holy fuck," I whisper to myself, just before Ava comes to a sudden stop. She starts the car, and floors it. The tires screech as the Nissan tears away and zooms past my house.

As she passes in front of me, Ava looks at my house and glares into the window. Although it should be improbable at that speed, I'm certain she looks right at me before she disappears from view.

TAKEOFF

CHAPTER THIRTY

Tessa ~

~ The sun seems brighter these days. The sky is bluer. The birds sing louder, and it feels like their song is just for me. Even now, as I take my seat at the bar in Applebee's, the place is nice and quiet, as if everyone in here knew I was in a calm and serene mood, and they all wanted to keep me in my happy place.

I've been on quite the rollercoaster lately, but I feel like I'm finally stepping off of the rocky ride and putting my feet on solid ground. My therapy session with Dr. Colson two days ago really solidified everything that was running through my mind.

I successfully climbed out of the basement my mother had me trapped in, and took my time exploring my newfound land of freedom. It was great, and I don't regret a single thing about anything I've done. If everything went down the same way, I wouldn't change a thing about how I reacted to being dumped. I'm better because of it, and I highly doubt Brandon can say the same.

I can't help but wonder how it all turned out for him,

though. I haven't heard anything about him or his band since he left town a few weeks ago, which is a bad sign for a band trying to come up. Maybe I'll never know, and that's perfectly fine with me.

The bar is quiet this evening, which is perfect. Missy is on her way, and we'll enjoy our usual girls night out with a few drinks and laughs. I guess the only thing that'll be different about tonight is that I won't be on the prowl.

After everything went down with my mother and Will—who I really hope isn't here tonight—something in me changed. Maybe all I needed was for my mother to leave me the hell alone and stop trying to get me to live my life by her outdated rules. That must've been it, because after we hugged that evening, everything seemed to slow down for me. I'm still living my life the way I want it, and if I wanted to sleep with somebody tonight I'd do it, but I don't feel the same sense of urgency. A lot of times, all we're really looking for is acceptance, and now that I've got hers, I'm good to take my time.

Once I'm seated and comfortable, I tell the bartender to hook me up with a vodka cranberry, and I take a big first sip as soon as he places it in front of me. As I'm putting my glass back on top of the napkin, I feel someone brush up against my arm as they sit down beside me. My first thought is that it's going to be Will looking for an explanation for what went down at the clinic with my mother. However, I'm surprised when I look over and see it's not Will. I don't remember this guy's name, but I definitely recognize his face.

He's a little on the thin side, with beautiful blue eyes, wavy hair, and a strong jaw. Once again, he's wearing a suit and standing out in the crowd of restaurant-goers. He has stubble on his face, but it looks really good on him, and when he looks at me, he flashes a gorgeous smile.

"Hey, I remember you," he says, flooring me with that smile. "Tessa, right? Tessa Milton."

I smile back and reach out to shake the hand that he has offered. "Yeah. I remember you, too, although I'm not sure what your name is."

"Ouch," he says with a playful chuckle. "It's Liam."

"Oh, right," I chirp. "Liam Gardner. Hi, it's nice to see you again."

It's *really* nice to see him again. Good lord, he's gorgeous.

"Nice to see you, too," Liam replies, before turning to the bartender and ordering a rum and coke and turning back to me. "So, how have you been?"

"I'm really good, thank you. How about you?"

"Much better than the last time I saw you," Liam says. "You definitely seem happier than last time, too. You've got a perky glow about you tonight. How about me? Am I glowing?"

A giggle escapes my throat. "I think you are."

"Oh, that's sweet of you to say. Well, I feel like I'm glowing for sure. Wanna know why?"

"Of course."

I'd listen to anything this man has to say, because I remember how easy it was to talk to him last time. I'd just decided to start acting like a grown, *single* woman, and Liam was here venting about how pushy his lawyer father was. I remember how good it felt to have someone to relate to, but before we could even connect, he finished his drink and was gone without a trace. It looks like fate has brought us together again.

"I signed the final papers to close on a new building today," Liam says with a broad, proud smile. He turns to sip his drink, but that grin never fades. It's so strong of a smile that it's contagious, making me smile, too.

"That's cool," I answer. "Still working business with your father?"

"Well, that's the *really* cool part about it, Ms. Milton," he says, and I instantly fall in love with how he says my name. "The papers we signed today were to close on a new building to house our new law firm. I took the bar exam, and now I'm starting my own firm with another lawyer friend of mine. It'll be called Liam and Rind. His name is William Rind, so it makes sense. Wait. It makes sense, right?"

Liam bulges his eyes when he looks at me and I giggle like a schoolgirl at his playfulness. He must've really been down in the dumps the last time we spoke, because he seems like a whole new man today. Much brighter and more alive. His smile is vibrant and flirtatious, and his sense of humor is on full display. It makes him even more attractive. Could he be any more perfect?

"Yes, it definitely does," I answer. "Well, I'm proud of you, Liam. That's awesome. Way to go."

Liam lets out a joyous chuckle before climbing out of his seat to take a bow in front of everyone in the restaurant. The bartender laughs and starts to applaud, causing three or four tables next to us to clap as well.

Liam twirls his hand in a circle and dips his head. "Thank you very much," he says, grinning from ear to ear. Apparently, getting out from underneath his father's thumb was exactly the relief he needed, and I love how much I can relate to that.

"All right, all right," Liam says as he sits back down. "Enough about how awesome I am, Tessa, geez. I get it, you like me. Let's just move on, all right?"

I let out another giggle with a shocked expression on my face.

"Uhh, all right. Somebody is really full of themselves today," I say, reveling in how good it feels to laugh and smile.

"I know, I'm sorry. It's just a really good day," Liam says. "But, enough about me. I want to hear about you. Last time I saw you, you were talking to me about your mother. How has that been going?"

He remembered. My heart does a little jig in my chest.

"Well, it was rough for a while, but it's better now," I tell him. "We had to have a real heart to heart, but we got it all out in the open. I told her how I felt about the way she was treating me, and she apologized. She hasn't been the same since. It's been so surreal that I'm still waiting for the day she goes back to how she used to be, but so far so good. It's been awesome."

"That's great! How do you feel now?"

"Like a thousand pounds has been lifted off my chest and shoulders, and I'm able to walk around free for the very first time. I feel like I'm floating, something you can relate to, I'm guessing."

"You're guessing right," Liam agrees. "I had a heart to heart with my dad, too. He didn't take it as well as your mother did, so we had to go our separate ways. Once I was free from him, I felt like I could fly to the moon and back, so I went ahead and kicked the bar exam's ass. Now, my firm will compete with my father's. Payback's a bitch."

Liam chuckles and sips his drink, pulling another smile from me. "You seem to be really enjoying your moment."

"I am! That guy has been a thorn in my side my entire life. I tried to do what you did. I tried to give him a chance to learn about how I felt and make adjustments, but he didn't want to do that. He's too hard-headed. So, I had to do what I had to do. All that matters now is that I'm happy. This feeling is irreplaceable. It can't be beat. Peace of mind means everything. I know you feel me on that one."

"I absolutely do."

"Yeah, I knew you would, Ms. Milton. That's why I like

you." Liam knocks back the rest of his drink and stands up. Watching him get up and prepare to leave gives me a sinking feeling in my stomach. I don't want to just let him go this time, but I feel nervous about asking him for his number, so I'll wait to see if he asks me for mine.

"All right, I've done enough celebrating tonight," Liam says. "Now I have to get to work so that the firm comes out swinging. So, I've got to go. It was great talking to you again, Tessa. Let's do it again soon."

"Yeah, we really should," I reply, hoping he takes the hint.

"All right. Have a good night," Liam says, before turning on his heel and walking out.

As he exits the restaurant, Missy comes strolling in, her red hair swinging behind her as she sits down next to me.

"Did you miss me?" she asks. "How long you been here?"

"Long enough to have a drink and some conversation," I answer, but I don't feel as chipper as I did a second ago.

"You okay," Missy asks. "You seem down."

"I'm fine. Let's get you a drink," I say. "Excuse me, bartender. Can we get her a..."

"Ms. Milton," I hear a voice call from behind me. I turn around to find Liam standing there, and my heart rate doubles.

"Listen, I have to be honest here," Liam begins. "I was sick the last time I left here without getting your number. I really enjoyed talking to you, and I think we can both get along and relate to each other in a way I'm not sure I've felt before. I couldn't just leave here a second time without asking if you're seeing anyone."

Missy and I both freeze, shocked by this turn of events. I could leap for joy right now.

"Umm, no. I'm not seeing anyone," I say, doing my best to keep my smile from overtaking my face.

"I don't know how something like that happens," Liam

says, shaking his head. "You're entirely too beautiful to be single. I was wondering if maybe I could have your number. Maybe we can go on a date and talk without me having to drink and run off so fast."

"Absolutely. I'd love that," I answer, and I can't put my number in his phone fast enough.

When it's all said and done, Liam smiles at me and Missy. "Awesome. Thank you. I'll give you a call soon."

"Can't wait," I answer, just before Liam turns and walks out.

As soon as he's gone, Missy turns to me with her mouth agape and her eyes wide. "Tell me *everything*!"

CHAPTER THIRTY-ONE

~ T essa ~

"Tessa, did you drop off the deposit last night?" my mother asks. She steps into my office wearing a white button-up and blue jeans, covered by a baby blue apron, but her clothes aren't what I focus on. It's the easy going smile she's wearing that I see first.

"Yeah, I did," I reply. I smile back, and instinctively wait for her to ridicule something about my appearance. My hair is down, and I didn't go all out on my makeup this morning. I was too tired for all of that, so maybe that's where she'll hit me. She keeps her eyes trained on me for a moment, and I expect her complaint to come spiraling at me like a missile any second now.

"Okay, I figured you did. Just wanted to make sure," she says, pinching her lips together, but keeping her smile intact. "Everything going okay with you, sweetie?"

"Yeah, everything's fine," I reply, and I think to leave it there, but another thought crosses my mind before my mother can walk out. "Actually, Mom, I've been thinking. You know, I'm always up to date on everything finance related around here. I've been doing this for so long that the system I have in place pretty much runs itself. I feel like I'm sort of bored sometimes, and I was considering taking on another account. One from another business."

My mother stares at me with no expression on her face, blinking a few times while she calculates what I just said.

"Would that affect you coming here?" she asks.

"Yeah, maybe a bit," I answer. "I was actually thinking about getting my own building. Some place I could manage a handful of accounts and have multiple streams of income. I'd have to grow it over time, and even hire a staff at some point, but I think I want to go into business for myself. Milton Animal Clinic would be my ribbon-cutting client. I'd never leave you guys behind, I just think I need to expand. What do you think?"

Judy lets out a breath, just before her face softens and she tilts her head to the side.

"I think that'd be great, Tessa," she says. "I really do. Your father and I would miss having you around here, but you're right. You've been here since you were just a teenager. You're a grown woman now, and you're absolutely smart enough to start your own business. I think it shows incredible growth. Your father and I will support you however you need us to. Just let us know how we can help."

"Wow," I say with raised eyebrows. "Thank you. I appreciate that very much."

"You're welcome," my mother says before turning on her heel. Before she walks away, she looks over her shoulder. "I'm very proud of you, Tessa."

In my chest, I feel a strong urge to cry. It stings like needles prickling underneath my rib cage. I don't even know where it came from, but it takes everything in me to swallow it back down just to be able to respond.

"Thanks, Mom," I reply. My mother flashes a soft but genuine smile just as she walks out.

Once she's gone, I pause a moment to think about how she's done such a dramatic turnaround. Is telling people how they make you feel really that powerful of a tool? It seems to have forced my mother into a complete reversal of how she used to be, and I'm so glad I took Dr. Colson's advice and spoke my truth to her. Well, it wasn't just Dr. Colson. I think my first conversation with Liam had a little something to do with it, too.

"Well, it seems that letting a guy fuck you from behind on the counter in the lobby is exactly the medicine your mom needed," Missy says as she waltzes into my office. Her red hair is tied into a tight ponytail, and her Delaware T-shirt matches the color of her apron, so they almost blend in together.

"Keep your voice down," I snip in a whisper. "Don't say that around her. I don't want it to trigger her into going back to being the most annoying person in my life. You're going to jinx it."

"Oh, excuse me. You're right." Missy comes in and takes a seat on the small black couch across from my desk. "So, you're about to branch out, huh? Gonna just leave me here to fend for myself."

I giggle. "Yeah, I think it's time. I didn't get a degree just to keep working at the same place I worked before I ever had a degree. But, you can work for me once I get it off the ground if you want."

"Aww," Missy says, placing her hand over her heart. "Just let me know when it's ready, and when you're offering extensive math classes for me to learn how to do shit with numbers, and I'm there."

We both chuckle together, before falling into silence. I think we both know big changes are coming. That kind of thing is always scary for everyone involved, but it's the right thing to do. It's going to take a lot of work, but I'm ready for it.

I think to vocalize my thoughts to Missy, but before I can speak, my cell phone vibrates on my desk. The number that comes across the screen isn't one I recognize, but it's a Delaware area code, so I decide to pick it up.

"Hello?" I say, and Missy starts to get up to leave so I can have some privacy.

"Hi, is this Tessa Milton?" Liam's voice booms from the phone loud enough for Missy to hear, and she pauses in the doorway.

"Yes, it is. Hi, Liam," I say as my eyes widen. I instantly feel a fresh surge of glee and adrenaline in my chest. Missy even does a little dance before she sits back down to be my perfectly nosey support system.

"So, you *did* give me the right number?" Liam says, and I can see his smile through the phone.

"I *did*," I reply.

"Well, thank you, Ms. Milton. How are you doing?"

Much better now!

"I'm good," I say, making sure I don't go overboard. "Really good, actually. How are you?"

"I'm great. Busy with work, but I'm still so thrilled with it that it doesn't really feel like work right now. I'm sure it will later, but for now, it's the best kind of busy in the world."

"I'm glad to hear it," I answer. I smile at Missy, and she reacts by forming a heart with her hands and mouthing "You're so cute," to me with a gigantic smile on her face.

"So listen," Liam goes on. "Now that I've mustered up the courage to call you and I see you didn't give me the wrong number, I was wondering if maybe you'd like to go on a date with me sometime soon. I've been dying to have some fantastic conversation with someone who listens and relates to me, and I think you might be the only person who can pull it off while also making it look *really* good."

I smile so big it hurts my face. "I'd love to."

"Great! Are you free later this evening?"

"I'll make sure I'm free whenever you'd like to meet up." Missy falls back in her chair and fans herself, and I roll my eyes as I smile.

"Okay, awesome," Liam replies. "How about seven-thirty? Ruby Tuesday in Milford sound okay?"

"It sounds great," I answer. The excitement I feel is almost too much to hold in any longer. "I'll see you then."

"See you then."

"Okay. Bye, Liam."

"Goodbye, Ms. Milton."

The second I hang up the phone and pull it away from my ear, my excitement breaks through the blockade, and Missy and I both erupt into childish screams of excitement.

CHAPTER THIRTY-TWO

~T essa ~

Liam smiles at me like he's seeing me for the first time, and he really likes what he sees. As a matter of fact, allow me to rephrase. Liam smiles at me like he's seen me a million times, and realizes how much he loves seeing me—like seeing me will never get old to him. The kicker is that this is only the third time we've seen each other. Liam just has this flicker of light in his eyes that shines like a star buried in his pupils, and the star brightens when he looks at me.

"What?" I ask as I begin to feel a little awkward from him staring.

"I don't know," Liam says, adjusting in his seat. "You're just nice to look at."

I can feel myself starting to blush, and I literally fan myself to keep my face from turning red. Sometimes, a simple compliment is the most effective.

This is the most dressed down I've ever seen Liam. The two times we ran into each other before, he was making a quick pit stop in Applebee's to have a drink to blow off some steam and celebrate an accomplishment, respectively. He was dressed in a nice suit every time, but tonight he's in a dark gray button-up with the top two buttons undone, revealing a toned chest with a barely-visible tattoo teasing just beneath the edge of the second button. I can't make out what the tattoo is from here, but my eyes are drawn to it. Liam is still fancy, but it's toned down. It doesn't change anything, though. He's as gorgeous as ever.

I chose to dine in a flowing black dress with silhouettes of flowers sweeping across the bottom. It's a little elegant, but it makes me feel gorgeous. These days, I'm all about doing what makes me feel good, regardless of what people may say about it. Life is too short to care about the opinions of strangers.

"So, how was work today? I've been curious about whether or not things held up for you the way you hoped they would," Liam says.

Our waitress brings our food and places it on the table. Liam ordered steak, while I chose two chicken breasts topped with asiago cheese and bacon.

"Well, I told my mother that I wanted to start my own business," I begin to explain before a sip of my ice water. "To my complete and utter surprise, she was very supportive. Even offered to help. So, I guess I'm branching out."

Liam nods his approval while swallowing down some steak smothered in A1 sauce. "Wow. That's incredible. I'm sure you're excited."

"For sure. I sort of stole a page out of your book on that one."

"Sounds like it," Liam says behind a smile. "I'm impressed, Ms. Milton. Staking your own claim. That's great."

"Thank you."

"I love how strong-minded you are," Liam says. The man has no sense of embarrassment when it comes to dishing out compliments. "You're focused, and you speak your mind. You don't see that enough from people, especially women, unfortunately. Personally, I think women should speak their minds more often, although I know society frowns on that kind of thing."

"Fuck society," I reply, stealing a line from Dr. Colson. Liam smiles like I just gave him a gift he's been wanting his entire life. "I don't mean to be so blunt... Well, yes I do. After everything I've gone through recently, including my breakup, I've found a ton of comfort in speaking my mind and doing things I want to do. There's no room for caring about other people's opinions to the point that it affects what I do."

"I hear that."

"So, when I tell you that I find you incredibly attractive, and that I keep wondering what that tattoo on your chest looks like without your shirt on, I mean it. I'm saying it because that's what I want to say."

Liam twists his mouth into a confused smirk.

"I don't mean to be too forward and come on too strong," I go on. "It's just the zone I'm in these days. Blame my therapist, but I'm just being honest. You're gorgeous, Liam, and I love how you keep putting a smile on my face. After dinner, I was hoping you could show me that tattoo while we lay in my bedroom."

I let the words linger in the air for a while, hoping I didn't just ruin a perfectly good date by being over-the-top. Liam, on the other hand, looks completely calm. He even grins before speaking again.

"Interesting," he says, nodding his head. "While I can totally appreciate that type of brutal honesty, I have to be honest myself. The truth is, Tessa, I think I might actually like you. Like, for real. After we met, I'm pretty sure I thought about you every single day until I saw you at the bar the second time. There's something about you I find very comforting and easy to talk to, and I appreciate that. So, when I asked for your number, it wasn't so I could try to get you in the sack for a one night stand. I wanted your number because I wanted to see where this could go in the long run. So, if it's okay with you, I'd like to take my time getting to know you. I mean, don't get me wrong, I'm not anti sex or anything like that. In fact, the thought of sex with you is doing something serious in my pants as we speak, but it's not all about that with me. I'm just interested in you *for real*. I'm not in any rush for anything specific. When we get to that point, and we *will* get to that point, I know it'll be incredible. It'll be earth-shattering. But I'd like to walk there, not run. Is that cool?"

Out of all the things I expected Liam to say, I never thought he'd say that. Any other guy would be trying to pay the check right now so we could go get started. Either that, or they'd call me a whore and try to use and abuse me. Not Liam, though. He actually wants to take his time getting to know me.

I may not have known what I wanted or liked until Brandon dumped me and I went and found my own voice. Everything may have had question marks before, but there's one thing I know for sure now—there isn't a person in the world who wouldn't like everything Liam just said. I don't have to sow any wild oats to know that I definitely want that.

I smile an uncontrollably large smile and nod my head. "Yeah, that's definitely cool."

MAINTENANCE

CHAPTER THIRTY-THREE

~M alcolm ~

Today is a great day. To me, there's no better feeling in the world than knowing a patient feels strong enough to move on in their life without you. It's monumental because it's a decision that isn't made by me. This comes directly from the patient, who decides in their own mind that they're ready to continue their lives, using the information we've gone over in our time together, and they feel bold and courageous. It's a proud parent kind of moment.

Tessa sits in front of me wearing all-black sweats, but nice ones. It's attire she wouldn't have worn before, because she felt she always had to be at the top of her game when she was with Brandon. He and Judy made Tessa feel like she always had to look her absolute best in order to be taken seriously in this world, which translated to being taken seriously by men. Now, however, Tessa has realized that she's allowed to be as comfortable as she wants to be. She can dress down or up, and as long as she feels beautiful, she *is* beautiful.

"So," I say to begin our session. "You've decided today will be the last time we see each other. I love that you feel confi-dent enough to move on from your therapy, but I'm curious what made you decide you'd like to be finished."

Tessa sweeps her hair off her shoulder, and even that movement seems more confident. I swear, Tessa is a completely different person than who I met with her ex, at a time that feels like it was years ago but was only a handful of weeks.

"Well, I think we've covered everything I needed to work my way through," Tessa says. "Plus, I'm at a place in my life where I don't want to be doing things that are still related to a version of me that no longer exists. I started coming here with Brandon so we could work on our relationship. When he dumped me, I kept coming because I was dealing with remnants of feelings and issues that were directly linked to him. Those remnants are gone now, and I don't want to keep being reminded of them week after week, although I like coming to talk to you. Lastly, I've met someone else, and we don't need therapy. I'm not ridiculing anyone who does need to see a therapist, but Liam and I don't, and hopefully we never will."

Tessa giggles, and I smile with her while I nod my head.

"I couldn't have said it better myself, Tessa," I say. "I agree with you one hundred percent. You're night and day different from when we met, and I think you're past the issues that first brought you here. I'm also proud to hear you say that you met someone else. Not to get into your business, but may I ask how things are going so far?"

"His name is Liam Gardner, and he's a lawyer," Tessa says, her face beaming with pride. "He just opened up his own law firm downtown, and he's amazing. He's thoughtful, brilliant, sexy, confident, and so unbelievably gorgeous. I think what I like about him most, though, is that he believes in me. He motivates me to do what I think is best for me, and he supports my decisions. Even more so, he wants to take his time with me.

"I'd be lying if I said I'm unaffected by the fact that we haven't had sex yet, but I'm cool with it. I love that he wants to slow things down and get to know me, and the more time goes by, the more I want him. It's almost like waiting is fore-play for us right now. I love it. I learn more and more every day, and the more I learn, the more I like him, and the more I like him, the more I want to be with him in every way."

"So, no sex yet," I repeat, wondering if Tessa is *really* okay with this setup.

"Not yet, but it'll happen soon," she says, and I don't sense any dissatisfaction in her voice. "It's like we're building up this tension, and when it does happen, it's going to be hot and lustful. Ugh, I can't wait."

"Lustful. Key word."

"That's right," Tessa says behind a chuckle.

"Well, I think you guys are headed for something special," I state. "It sounds like you're on the right path, and I'm happy and excited for you. You know what your relationship needs are now, and I think you're strong enough to make sure they're being met by your partner. You're going to do just fine, Tessa. I know it. You made the right decision when you decided to take time to get to know yourself. In fact, I have a little surprise for you."

"A surprise?"

I get up from my chair and walk over to my desk, where I pull a newspaper clipping from my drawer. I bring it over to Tessa and hand it to her. The smile that overtakes her face is brilliant.

"Oh, my god!" she barks, just before falling into a fit of laughter.

"Consider it a going away present," I say with a proud smile on my face. "I saw that in the paper a few days ago and thought you'd get a kick out of it. Apparently, American Armpits was being booed off the stage in Philly, and decided to try to fight some people in the audience. All of the band members—including their manager slash producer, Brandon Stills—were arrested and charged with inciting a riot, and disorderly conduct. They also got their asses beaten by some members of the audience before they were locked into their cuffs."

Tessa and I share a laugh at the expense of her ex, and although it's probably a bit unethical, I enjoy the moment. Brandon isn't a current patient, so fuck it.

"I just wanted you to see that you definitely made the right decision," I say after we stop laughing. Tessa's mouth is still curled into an entertained smile. "Brandon will probably be back in Dover soon, and if you two run into each other, he'll see that you have moved on and upgraded yourself and your life without him. If he hasn't already realized how much he messed up, he definitely will soon."

"Wow, that's so funny. Thanks for showing me this. I mean, I'll probably throw it in the trash because I don't ever want to think about him again, but I really appreciate this."

I get up from my seat and take the clipping from Tessa's hands. I let her watch me ball it up and toss it in the trash can behind my chair before I sit back down. "Done."

"Well, I really want to thank you for everything, Dr. Colson," Tessa says. She locks her eyes on me and her face turns serious. "You've been incredible, and I really appreciate all of your support during this chaotic period in my life. You've really got a way with words, and you're amazing at making me feel empowered. You're a true feminist, and I think it's awesome."

"Feminist? I wouldn't say I'd label myself a feminist. I just think there are a lot of double standards out there that are completely unfair to women. Basically, all I want is for women to be respected and held to the same standards as men. I understand there may be physical differences in size and strength, but morally, ethically, and financially women deserve the same respect as men. To be blunt, men get a pass on a lot of bullshit, and it's not fair. I just want it to be equal, and I aim to empower my patients to be the change the world needs."

"I hate to break it to you, Dr. Colson," Tessa says, and I can see a laugh ready to erupt from her. "But that's *exactly* what a feminist is."

"Oh," I say, fighting back a smile. "Well, then I guess I'm a feminist."

The two of us laugh together once again, and my final session with Tessa Milton ends on a perfect high note.

CHAPTER THIRTY-FOUR

~ Malcolm ~

My life has been a journey, to say the least. I'm a relationship and sex therapist who's great at giving advice, but not at taking it. I guess that's fitting. If I had to sit myself down on my own couch and talk to myself, I'd say I have a problem that needs to be addressed as soon as possible, and it has nothing to do with how I treat my patients. It's all about how I treat myself.

I know Ava is bad for me, but in the few days since I spoke to her last, I've had moments where I felt like I would die if I didn't have her. I don't mean that in a way that suggests I miss her or love her. When I say I needed to have her, I mean I felt like I was going through withdrawals due to the lack of sex.

I'm aware I could put myself out there to meet someone new. I could meet a nice woman in a bar in Philly, or drive down to DC for a night on the town, and maybe I could even hook up with someone here in Dover. I'm not above one-night stands, by any means. I know I could still have an active sex life if I wanted to. That's not the problem. My problem is that it's Ava I want to have sex with, because nobody fucks the way we did.

Ava was the perfect submissive, and I'm the kind of man who *needs* a submissive. I crave the control that comes with it, and I'm obsessed with watching a woman orgasm from my touch. It's what makes me who I am. I could try to fuck in the vanilla way the majority of the world does, but my dominance comes naturally. Fighting it is like telling myself I don't have to breathe in order to live. I do have to breathe. I do have to be dominant.

When I see my hard work and expertise paying off in the form of Tessa Milton or Sean Tillman, I can't help but be proud. Therapy helps people in so many ways, and all it takes is for the person to admit they need help and to seek it out. Admitting you need help is almost always the hardest part, and maybe that's why this is so hard for me.

Am I an addict? Am I unable to control how badly I crave Ava? It must be the case, because who else would willingly accept all of the baggage that comes with her? Why subject myself to her issues and instability? As her former therapist, I knew her issues were bound to resurface sooner or later, but I went for it anyway. What does that say about me?

It says I was literally willing to place myself in harms way in order to get what I wanted, and that was sex with my perfect submissive. I was willing to risk things becoming too much for me to handle, and allowed myself to dive in with her, knowing it wouldn't lead anywhere good. I *knew* it was never going to be anything long term, and I did it anyway. This is the behavior of addicts. This is how people who need help making the right decisions typically act, and that's a tough pill to swallow.

When I reach my driveway, I pull in and put the car in park. Overall, today was a good day. I left my office knowing Tessa would go on and have a great life with her new boyfriend. I'm filled with nothing but hope when it comes to her, and I believe she's going to do great. My life, however, needs a little maintenance.

As I climb out of the car, I'm hit with a fresh Dover breeze. The wind gently caresses my face, and I feel at ease as I start towards the front door. The sun is still out, and Delaware has decided to gift us with sixty-degree weather in the middle of February. It's a good day to self-evaluate and make changes for the better. When I get inside, I know which phone call I have to make. I'm admitting I need help, and now I have to seek it out.

As I approach the front door, I fumble with my keys before finding the right one. I could've just gone in through the garage, but sometimes I like stepping out into the weather and feeling the elements on my face. It's the small things that tend to make us the happiest.

As I push the key into the slot, I hear an engine rev up behind me and I instinctively glance back. When I see the car, my heart jumps in my chest, slamming into my rib cage like a deranged mental patient in a padded room.

It's a dark Nissan, and it's a few houses down. It approaches slowly, creeping closer while I stand in front of my door, frozen in place.

Ava.

What do I do when Ava approaches me? What do I say? Does she want sex or to set my house on fire like her last boyfriend? If she wanted sex, am I strong enough to turn her down right now? After the week I've had, I'm not sure I'd be able to turn her away if she wanted to go down into the Black House. Damn, I miss the Black House.

The car moves closer and I feel a little lightheaded.

Fuck.

What should I do?

What will she say?

How will I respond?

The Nissan reaches my driveway and I focus my eyes on the driver. I lean forward and squint until I can make out the person. My breath is stuck in my throat as my vision clears, and I realize it's not her. Ava isn't behind the wheel, and the car keeps on driving right past my house.

Slowly, my heartbeat dwindles down to its normal pace. My breathing returns to its natural state, and my muscles relax.

It wasn't her, after all. Maybe she has moved on. There was a part of me that didn't think she would without causing a problem first, but maybe it's me who needs to do what Ava has done, and move on with my life.

As I turn around and open my front door, I step inside and plan to leave my addiction to Ava outside with the unusually warm breeze. The door will close behind me, and so will the chapter of my life that included Ava Pierson.

Tomorrow, I will start anew.

THE END

TURN THE PAGE FOR CHAPTER ONE OF THE FALLOUT (THE THERAPIST #3)

~ Demi ~

He sits next to me smelling of a masculine, seductive cologne, but the stench of the past is what captivates me. My husband, Eli Lane, is what dreams are made of. He's sexy, a thick one hundred eighty pounds of masculinity and strength. His shoulders are broad, his beard thick, his voice deep and commanding. Physically, he's everything I ever wanted. He's everything anybody could want.

"So, what'd you think?" he asks, his mouth lifted into a playful smile, continuing the good mood he's been in all evening. That's another thing about Eli I've always loved. His sense of humor is perfect—an impeccable combination of funny and flirtatious.

"It was amazing," I reply, my smile soft and genuine. It's also forced.

"Thank you," Eli says. "It was the least I could do for someone who's as stunning as you. I love you, Demi."

Tears begin to sting my eyes, threatening to breach the contract we'd signed before the evening started saying I wouldn't show how much I'm crying on the inside. I fight them back as I lick my lips and look Eli in his blue eyes.

"Thank you for dinner. I loved it."

It comes out choppy and staccato, but it's the best I can do. I've gotten really good at acting lately, and when Eli leans in to kiss me, I put on another Oscar-worthy performance by tilting forward and pressing my lips against his. Like it doesn't bother me. Like it doesn't feel like a vice gripping my entire body in its jaws.

"All right, what do you say I get this cleaned up and we cap it off with some wine?" Eli asks. He sounds like he doesn't expect me to say yes, so when I nod my head, his smile is filled with relief and excitement.

I stay at the glass dinner table while Eli lifts the plates of leftover salmon off and walks them into the kitchen. I watch him go, marveling at how attractive my husband is. I can't speak for every woman, but my guy is stunning, and has been since the moment I met him at a bar here in Rehoboth, Delaware. I was there with two of my girlfriends from the office, and Eli walked in with two of his friends from his job. I remember the moment he walked in because he stood out from the crowd of guys trying to look good. Eli and his crew weren't trying to look good. They were just there to have a drink and blow off some steam, wearing an assortment of flannel shirts and dark blue jeans. His friend's beards were long and scruffy, but Eli's face was smooth. The group looked strange, like Eli was the celebrity and the guys with him were his bodyguards. The moment I saw him, I was instantly his, even if he didn't know it yet.

I remember how they walked in a triangle, with Eli right in the front. He was the point, the leader of the group, and he looked the part. His posture overflowed with confidence, and the way his eyes swept across the bar as he searched for the bartender certainly caught my eye, because as he looked for the bartender, he spotted me. We locked eyes, smiled at each other, and he left his friends behind to come sit next to me. He didn't even order a drink. I was all he saw. He was all I saw. My friends disappeared into the fuzzy background of people and voices while Eli and I talked amongst ourselves, as if life had shined a spotlight on the two of us. We've talked every day since then. Every single day.

He's still that man. Even now, as he stands over the sink wearing a similar red and black flannel shirt, looking like the posterboy for domestication while he washes dishes after having cooked dinner for his wife. Marrying me didn't change the allure. He's still unbelievably sexy, masculine, and perfect. He still commands attention.

"So, shall I bring over the entire bottle, or are we just going with glasses?" he says with a chuckle, and I smile back.

"Umm, glasses will do. Just fill mine to the very top. If you don't struggle to keep it from spilling, you haven't filled it enough."

"Too much wine to keep it all in the glass is the perfect amount," he replies in that quick-witted way he does. "Since we're both off work tomorrow, I think I'll fill mine the same way. Maybe we can knock off the entire bottle between the two of us. You up for the challenge?"

I'm not dumb, although I've kept myself up many nights questioning whether that's true or not. I know what Eli is doing, and I decide to go along with it.

"Sure, let's see if we can do it." I swallow hard, watching as the corners of Eli's mouth lift once again.

I move into the living room, sitting on the cream-colored loveseat in front of the ivory coffee table. The fireplace crackles in front of me beneath the eighty-inch TV mounted on the wall. Eli brings two glasses of wine and sets them both on the table in front of me. Ironically, a bit of red wine glides down the side of my glass and forms a tiny puddle on the table.

"Look at that. The perfect amount," Eli says. He lifts his glass and takes a big gulp, before looking at me with expectation in his eyes. I see hope and pleading in his face as he watches me.

When I look at the wine-filled glass, I see more than just wine. I see Eli's desire to move on. I see his need for normalcy. I see it as a big red question mark, and the question is whether or not I'm ready to move on. Am I ready to let go? Am I able to get back on the road we've been on since that day in the bar when we saw each other and made the entire room disappear, leaving nothing but the two of us together. Am I ready?

My heart feels like each beat is that of a bass drum, pounding in my chest, rattling my rib cage. My nerves are sensitive, and the urge to cry is just as strong now as it was before, and I know everything will always be this way if I don't push through it and move on. I have to fight past this feeling, and force us back on track. I must overcome it, and the first step is picking up the wine glass. I must answer the question.

Before the urge to withdraw can consume me, I exhale, pick up the glass, and take two large gulps that drain the alcohol by half. I don't even put the glass back on the table. I keep it in my hand, ready for the next big drink.

"So," I begin, still feeling nervous. "How was work?"

ACKNOWLEDGMENTS

Book two is complete! Wow, another amazing journey where I finally said things I've wanted to say for so long. It feels good to be able to talk about things that are important to you, and that's why *The Therapist* is changing how I feel about writing books.

I've always labeled myself a feminist. It's probably strange to some people because I'm active duty military, which is heavily dominated by men and testosterone. Somehow, I'm a little bit of an anomaly because I think the world is fucked up and women don't get the respect they deserve.

I'm not here to bash men, and that wasn't the intent of *Shameless (The Therapist #2)*, but I'm definitely here for empowering women in all the ways men are empowered. I have the amazing privilege of having a daughter, and I want her to know she has the right to do whatever she wants, the same way men do, and that's why Tessa was brought to life.

I'm in the middle of writing this series right now. It's amazing because as I write these acknowledgements, I actually finished with the manuscript for *The Fallout (The Therapist #3)* today as well. I'm making a ton of progress, and I've been sort of keeping to myself while writing this series, so the list of people I have to thank is quite short. Let's knock it out so I can get back to editing.

As usual, the first person I have to thank is the most important person in my life, and that's my wife. As I write this, only you and I know what is going into these books and how much thought we've had to put into them. I'm writing the series, but there really is a lot of us on the pages. I've bounced tons of ideas off of you and will continue to do so as Malcolm embodies both of us. We're using him to teach others, and I appreciate your input throughout this process. Thanks, baby. I love you.

I'd also like to thank my parents for all of their support, both directly and indirectly. This is going to be a huge summer when this series starts dropping, and I already know my parents are going to be out there with paperbacks putting in work. I love you guys.

To my brother, Shawn, I fucking love you, man. I wish I was physically there to help you through the shit you're going through right now, but I'm with you in spirit, and if you need absolutely anything, you know I got you. Darrion, I love you, too. You're not alone.

I'd like to thank everyone at Give Me Books, especially Jo, for all the help and promo for this book release. At the time of this writing, we haven't gotten started promoting all of this, and I know it's a task to promote four books over a four-month span, but I can't wait to see this machine in action.

Thank you to all of my beta readers. Thank you to all of the fans who've flocked to my page with words of encouragement and excitement about this series. This is the greatest thing I've ever done, and I know you won't be disappointed. If the betas from *The Therapist (The Therapist #1)* are any indication, this is about to be massive.

Can we finally surpass the tidal wave that hit when *Kingpin (An Italian Mafia Romance)* came out? Fingers crossed, because this series deserves it. I know this is subjective, but as the writer of all my work I'm telling you this series is the best thing I've ever done. I think it's also the most important. I can't wait until it's out for the world to see and spread.

Lastly, if you're reading this book, thank you! I love you. Enjoy the journey.

Represent...

MORE FROM WS GREER

More From WS Greer

Thank you for purchasing *Shameless (The Therapist #2)*! Please leave an honest rating and review wherever you purchased your copy. It'd be very much appreciated!

Check out these other titles from WS Greer...

Frozen Secrets (A Detective Granger Novel)
Claiming Carter (The Carter Trilogy #1)
Becoming Carter (The Carter Trilogy #2)
Destroying Carter (The Carter Trilogy #3)
Defending Her
Kingpin (An Italian Mafia Romance #1)
Long Live the King (An Italian Mafia Romance #2)
Red Snow (A Detective Granger Novel)
Madman (Love & Chaos #1)
Boss
The Therapist (The Therapist #1)
Shameless (The Therapist #2)

The Fallout (The Therapist #3)
Toxic (The Therapist #4)

Want more from WS? Follow him everywhere!
https://www.facebook.com/AuthorWSGreer
http://wsgreer.wordpress.com/
https://www.goodreads.com/author/show/7044361.W_S_Greer
https://twitter.com/AuthorWSGreer